DRY GULCH REVENGE

Hank Hawkins has the opportunity to achieve his ambition of buying a ranch. All he has to do is help a gang rob the stage in the Devil's Bones canyons. But it turns out the bandits never intended to leave anyone alive — including him . . . Upon regaining consciousness, Hawkins vows to track down the murderers who betrayed him. But when he sets off, he has a companion accompanying him: Helen Curtis, the fiancée of the messenger whose death lies heavy on Hawkins' conscience.

Books by Clay More
in the Linford Western Library:

RAW DEAL AT PASCO SPRINGS
A ROPE FOR SCUDDER
STAMPEDE AT RATTLESNAKE PASS

CLAY MORE

DRY GULCH
REVENGE

Complete and Unabridged

LINFORD
Leicester

First published in Great Britain in 2014 by
Robert Hale Limited
London

First Linford Edition
published 2017
by arrangement with
Robert Hale
an imprint of The Crowood Press
Wiltshire

A catalogue record for this book is available
from the British Library.

ISBN 978–1–4448–3343–0

Published by
F. A. Thorpe (Publishing)
Anstey, Leicestershire

Set by Words & Graphics Ltd.
Anstey, Leicestershire
Printed and bound in Great Britain by
T. J. International Ltd., Padstow, Cornwall

This book is printed on acid-free paper

To Walt, my running buddy.

1

The sun beat down from a cloudless cobalt sky, parching every living thing that was unfortunate enough to be exposed to its relentless blaze. For the travellers both on top and inside the Concord as it lurched along the semi-desert trail, through tracts of sand and towering red rock formations, then across gigantic boulder-strewn plains where only mesquite and saguaro cactus thrived, the heat seemed well-nigh unbearable. Those inside were afforded some shade, yet the glassless windows meant that they accumulated a fine patina of dust.

'Hey driver, how long until the next stop?' yelled one of the inside passengers as he leaned as far out of the window as he could. 'We're dying of thirst in here.'

Hank Hawkins grinned as he handled

the team of six horses with the ease of an expert. He was a tall, well-built man with laughing green eyes and black hair that kept escaping from under his aged Stetson to hang over his eyes. He had a whip by his side and a canteen by his left foot, which he had drunk sparingly from — just enough to keep his mouth moist in the blistering heat.

Although he had explained to each passenger that they would have twenty miles between each stage of their journey, when they would stop at either a way station or a swing station, there was always at least one who either wouldn't listen or failed to comprehend what he had said. At the way station they could expect to get down and have time to eat a meal or take care of bodily essential functions. On the other hand, at a swing station they would literally have a mere fifteen minutes or so while the driver and the swing hostler changed the team. He had emphasized that it was going to be a hot trip and that it was up to each person to sort out their own drinks.

'We're stopping at the swing station in about one mile,' Hank shouted a reply. 'Just about time to get some water from the pump there.'

There was a snort of contempt from the passenger. 'Water! I need me some coffee, not goddamned water.'

Hank turned to Tom Burton, the messenger sitting on his left, and winked. 'I reckon that whiskey drummer wouldn't be quite so thirsty if he stopped trying to wash the trail dust off his tonsils with some of his samples.'

Tom laughed. 'Yeah, I sure hope he doesn't try lighting up a cigar or he could blow us and hisself to kingdom come.'

There were three passengers sitting behind them on the rooftop seats of the Concord. One was a preacher, another was an Irish miner named O'Leary, with huge bulging biceps and a ruddy, cheerful face. The last was a wrangler who had allowed no one to touch the Texas rig saddle that was all too obviously his most cherished possession.

'Amen to that,' said Eli Tabner, the preacher, a mellow-looking fellow in his late thirties with wire-framed spectacles perched on a thin nose under a floppy felt hat. 'I had to vacate my seat inside because of the fumes emanating from his mouth every time he talked or snored.' He coughed politely. 'Not to mention his profanity! I remonstrated with him twice, but he just scoffed at me and asked why it bothered me, especially since there were no ladies present.'

'Maybe he thought you was some sort of woman, preacher,' quipped the wrangler, who had merely introduced himself upon taking his seat, as Dusty. He pulled out his makings and started to build a cigarette.

O'Leary the Irishman prodded him with his knee. 'Why sure you must have been out in the sun too long, my friend, if you are thinking that the preacher here looks like a woman. He's prettier

4

than a lot of women, I grant you, but personally I prefer my ladies to look more — buxom.'

The preacher glared at them as they burst into a chorus of laughter. He muttered something under his breath then pulled out a battered bible and opened it at a well-thumbed page. He pushed his spectacles further up the bridge of his nose and began to read.

Inside the coach there were three passengers including the whiskey drummer, who after taking a swig of a sample bottle had once more fallen into a doze permeated by the odd snore. The two men sitting opposite him had used up all of their polite conversation after a half-day's enforced companionship.

At the start of their journey they had each volunteered information about themselves. The younger of the two, Gaston Legrand, a portly man in his early thirties, dressed in a brand new suit, starched shirt and tie, and sporting a moustache that had been beeswaxed and twirled into points in the European style, had volunteered that he was a chef, trained in Paris, France. After running a successful restaurant in New York he had decided to go west and introduce fine cuisine to the frontier. He had recounted in mouth-watering detail some of the recipes that he planned to put on his menu.

His fellow traveller was older and had the look of a professional gambler, which went with the name he had divulged, Barclay Parker. He too seemed to have travelled and was familiar with various eateries, restaurants and hotels back east, as well as all manner of establishments in the west. To their mutual delight they spent a long time talking about good food, fine wines and the pleasure of brandy and a good cigar.

The whiskey drummer had at that point launched enthusiastically into the virtues of good American sipping whiskey and emphasized his sales pitch by producing sample bottles from his travelling bag. When his offers of whiskey were refused he had started to imbibe himself, his voice becoming gradually more slurred and his language less wholesome. When they stopped at the way station for a meal and the preacher had taken the opportunity to relocate himself atop the coach, the drummer had taken the opportunity to sprawl himself across the whole bench.

Neither Legrand nor Parker had a good word to say about the state of the meal they had received and having no more to say to each other they both had been lulled off to sleep by the lurching motion of the Concord.

A high-pitched whistle from Hank Hawkins was followed by a shout.

'Get ready folks! The swing station is just up ahead. We'll be stopping for no more than fifteen minutes; just long enough to tend to any personal matters. But be quick, there's only one outhouse and you'll have to queue. Anyone who's not on the stage at the end of those fifteen minutes will need

7

to wait over for a day.'

* * *

Hank and Abe Purcell, the grizzly old swing station hostler, took exactly thirteen minutes to change the team.

'You said fifteen minutes and by golly you did it with time to spare,' observed Tom Burton as Hank pulled the Concord out of the swing station back on to the trail. 'Let's hope it's not unlucky thirteen, Hank.'

'Why'd you say that?' Hank snapped. Then, as if aware of his reaction his face broke into a grin. He was usually renowned for his cheerful demeanour.

'Hey, Hank, take it easy,' Tom returned. 'You seem a mite edgy today. 'I was just timing you.'

'Sorry, Tom. I guess I just want to get on and haul the stage through the Devil's Bones, but especially through the Devil's Knee. It's a tricky drive along those tight bends.' He nodded at the watch in Tom's hand. 'But as for timing me, I guess you just wanted to drool over that picture you keep inside that watch of yours.'

Tom glanced at his open pocket watch and grinned at the miniature portrait of Helen Curtis, that smiled out at him from the inside cover.

'Just another day, darling, then I'll see you again,' he said aloud. 'Reckon I'll be able to kiss you properly then.' And so saying, he raised the watch to his lips and kissed the image before snapping the watch closed and replacing it in his vest pocket. His fingers rested on the chain for a moment, then they settled on the stock of the shotgun that he had cradled across his knees.

'Well what do you know,' said O'Leary. 'The messenger has a goddess in his watch. A real beauty! I caught a glimpse of her myself.'

Tom turned and grinned. 'She is truly that. She painted that little picture for me her own self. She's educated and talented. She's an artist and a damned fine teacher that I mean to ask to marry me when I next see her.'

Dusty the wrangler guffawed. 'I hope you've got plenty of stamina, son. That filly looks like she may have spirit. And I reckon you need to buy her a ring. Fifty bucks and you can have this one,' he said, holding out his right hand to show a large, thick signet ring with a bronco motif.

Tom laughed. 'I think I'll be giving her something a bit more dainty than that.'

The Reverend Tabner leaned over and laid a hand on Tom's shoulder. 'I saw your young lady, too, sir. She is indeed a beauty to behold. And if you don't mind me saying, I am pleased that you are planning to marry, to sanctify your union under God's eye.'

'Thanks, preacher,' Tom replied. 'Helen is the perfect woman as far as I am concerned. A woman worth dying for.'

He didn't notice the worried look that Hank flashed him.

★　★　★

The Rio Pintos Stagecoach Company proudly boasted that it was the fastest passenger and delivery service in and around the Pintos Mountains. Its motto 'None Faster, None Safer' was painted in fancy gold letters above the company's name on each of the Concord's doors. Hank Hawkins had worked for the company for three years and was reckoned to be one of their most experienced drivers, but even he always felt slightly apprehensive about the drive round the Devil's Knee.

Five miles after the swing station the trail left the desert and entered the foothills of the Pintos Mountains, zigzagging between the boulders and red rock mesas before the land changed again and it entered the network of canyons known as the Devil's Bones. There were actually dozens of these canyons, many of which were box canyons, so the names of the skeleton's joints were given to those that the trail snaked its way through. The Devil's Knee was particularly notorious for it was a real zigzag canyon in which the trail ran along a narrow ledge hugging one side of the canyon, while the other side fell away into a ravine forty or fifty feet deep.

Negotiating the bends had to be virtually done at walking pace with the driver controlling and keeping the horses from getting too skittish. And since the ledge along which the trail ran was too narrow for two stagecoaches to pass there was a crude sign well in advance of each end advising travellers to fire off a shot or holler to alert anyone coming in the opposite direction.

'OK, Tom, best let anyone know we're here,' Hank said, as he tightened his hold on the reins and began the descent into the first stretch of the Devil's Knee.

* * *

The shot had echoed eerily around the network of canyons. Everyone on board the Concord had tensed up as the trail began to narrow and the chasm opened up on the right. It took all of Hank's skill to coax the team along the ledge, despite their blinkered vision.

'Holy smoke!' gasped the Irishman. 'I can see why they call this the Devil's Knee. If there was smoke coming out of that pit I'd believe we were walking past the doorway to hell itself.'

'There may not be smoke, but it sure is as hot as hell,' agreed Dusty, the wrangler.

'Gentlemen, please,' the preacher protested. 'It does no good to joke about Satan's abode. We should look to the Lord. If you want I could lead you all in a prayer.'

Hank let out a curse as he slowed the team even more as they negotiated the first sharp bend of the Devil's Knee. 'If it's all the same with you, preacher,' he said between grated teeth, 'I'd as soon just concentrate on getting us round the

Devil's Knee in one piece.'

The preacher ignored him and began to pray, raising his voice to do so.

'Our Father, which art in heaven, lead us . . . '

'Tom!' Hank snapped. 'Shut him up, will you. I can't afford to be distracted right now. One false move and we could go over the side.'

Tom stared dubiously at him. 'Are you all right, Hank? You've done this run a hundred times before. What's made you so jittery?'

The preacher's voice seemed to quake and grow louder. ' . . . give us this day our holy bread, and forgive us . . . '

'Just do it, Tom!' Hank demanded. 'Now!'

Tom shrugged and turned round to remonstrate with the preacher.

Suddenly, a shot rang out, followed by a series of echoes which made it sound as if a whole fusillade had been fired off up ahead.

Hank hauled on the reins, and

brought the team to a halt. Ahead of them, standing in the middle of the trail was a gunman with a Winchester Repeater aimed at them. He was dressed in a duster coat, with his hat pulled well down and a bandanna up to conceal the lower part of his face.

'Hands up, all of you,' he snapped. 'And you inside, come out real slow . . . '

Tom spun round, his jaw falling open in momentary astonishment. Then he snapped his mouth closed and swung the double-barrelled shotgun round.

The gunman's Winchester barked and Tom's body was thrown backwards as a bullet hammered into his chest, causing a fountain of bright red blood to splatter over Hank.

'No!' Hank cried as he tried to reach for Tom's lifeless body as it slumped down and his hands fell away from the shotgun.

'I warned him!' the gunman snarled. 'Now all of you, get your damned hands up.'

'T-take it easy, mister,' stammered the wrangler.

'No need to shoot,' agreed the Irishman.

The preacher had gone silent and was staring at the gunman, his bible shaking in his hands.

The door of the Concord was thrown open and the whiskey drummer poked his head out. 'Hey! Please don't shoot. We're just a bunch of poor travellers on our way . . . .'

The barrel of a gun appeared over the drummer's shoulder and instantly a shot was fired at the gunman.

'Take that you bastard,' yelled Barclay Parker.

But the shot went wide.

The gunman suddenly laughed. 'You asked for it!' he yelled.

Hank stared in horror as he saw the gunman take a couple of swift sideward paces so that he was standing almost on the edge of the ledge. In doing so he had opened up his line of vision and he fired, working the lever

16

action to fire again and again into the Concord.

'No! Stop, please!' Hank yelled.

He heard the cries of agony from down below and saw the top of the whiskey drummer's head almost explode to scatter blood and brain matter all over the side of the Concord. And he heard rather than saw the bodies of the other two men being hurled back into the interior of the Concord as the Winchester spat death.

'Get the shotgun,' the Irishman cried at Hank, as he tried to shift Tom's body to reach the fallen weapon.

Then another gun started firing, from somewhere behind and up above the Concord, as if from some vantage point atop the canyon wall. The Irishman cried out once as two bullets hit him in the back and he slumped forward over Tom's body.

'Don't shoot!' cried the wrangler, spinning round with his hands in the air, pleading to this previously unknown second gunman.

Hank felt his horror rapidly transformed into anger and the desire to kill. He dived for Tom's shotgun, plucked it up and swung it round to try to blast the first gunman off the ledge into the hellish chasm beyond.

But before he could pull the trigger he heard more gunfire and more screams. Then he felt an explosive pain in his head, then nothing more.

He pitched off the Concord on to the trail and his blood began to soak the ground round his head.

2

The woman's voice sounded angelic.

Hank Hawkins had never been a religious man. Although he generally went to church at least once a month he had never been particularly convinced by any of the preachers who had sermonized at the congregation about the blessings of heaven and the damnation of hell. From his own experience he reckoned that there really was no such thing as good and evil, there was just the ways of men. And most men seemed to have a measure of both good and bad in them.

Vague thoughts about good and evil hovered in his mind and he tried to follow each thought, but failed. Everything seemed jumbled up and he felt as if he was floating in a huge black cauldron of gloom. He felt disgusted with himself. He felt horrified, but he was not sure why.

Then pictures started to form, of men with blood spouting out of bullet wounds. And then he heard cries of agony and screams of pain.

The Devil's Knee! The name flickered through his mind. Then he had an image of a dark chasm.

Hell itself.

That was it, he had fallen into hell and he was paying the price for all of his sins.

Then he heard the angel's voice again, calling his name. It was the sweetest sensation he ever had. It seemed as if an angel was calling him back from the jaws of death, saving him from hell.

And then he felt the pain in his head and felt the build-up of a wave of nausea. His mind started flashing images before him. He saw Tom open his watch and show him the picture of his girl.

Then he heard him say: 'She's worth dying for, Hank.'

Almost immediately he heard a shot and saw Tom's body being thrown back and blood spurting everywhere. He started to thrash about, trying to force these awful images away.

Her voice broke through again, reassuring him, telling him that he was safe. That he was with friends.

He forced his eyes open and saw her — the angel behind the angelic voice. Despite himself, he gasped, for he thought her the most beautiful woman he had ever seen in his life — or in his death, if indeed he was now dead.

Slowly his thoughts started to clarify and he realized that he was not dead at all. The angel was looking down at him all right, but he now knew that she was a flesh and blood woman. A woman who was looking at him with concern in her eyes, in her expression and in her very demeanour.

It was Tom's Helen and she looked as if she was worried about him.

That wasn't right. That was not how it should be, Hank told himself.

Especially not when Tom was dead.

And it was all Hank's fault that they were all dead.

He heard himself scream as a wave of dizziness made his vision go blurred and he felt himself fall, down and down into a deep black hole.

'I deserve to be dead!' he moaned, as he imagined himself spinning down into the bowels of hell itself.

★　★　★

A bird was singing and the air smelled of freshly baked apple pie and lavender blossom when Hank awoke. He forced his eyes to open, only to immediately shut them again, for sunlight was streaming through a window and it hurt. Then he felt the dull headache again, but mercifully, this time there was no nausea. He waited a few moments then slowly allowed his eyes to flutter open.

He was alone in a comfortable room, which seemed to be in someone's house rather than a hotel. There was a large bunch of lavender in a vase by the open window. On a table were his clothes, neatly folded, with his Stetson on top. An armchair was at the side of the bed and on a bedside table an open book lay beside a sketchpad.

He pushed himself up to a sitting position, and then sidled back to rest against the bank of pillows. He turned his head to get a better look at the sketchpad, then gasped. Picking it up he saw that someone had made a sketch of himself lying asleep.

'Damn! Is that what I look like?' he said to himself. 'You wouldn't know if I was asleep or dead.'

He felt a shiver run up his spine as he said the words, for the horror of the ambush flooded into his mind. He dropped the sketchpad on the bedcovers and covered his face with his hands.

How many of them died in the ambush? He knew that Tom and the whiskey drummer had definitely died.

O'Leary looked as if he had almost certainly bought it, after being shot twice in the back. But what about the others?

'Any which way you look at it, it was all my fault,' he said to himself. 'It was all because of me.'

And his mind went back to the meeting he had with Wilson, the man who had promised him that the robbery would go smoothly and that no one would get hurt. Apart from taking the passengers' wallets, guns and whatever they had in their pockets, all that he would take would be the Hagsworth Bank strongbox that was locked up in the Concord's boot.

The Devil's Knee would be a perfect place for the hold-up, since it was on a ledge and no one could get past the stage to pursue the robber. All that Hank had to do was act dumb, make sure that the messenger surrendered his weapon and that the passengers did likewise.

When it came to it, he hadn't had

time to stop Tom from doing what he had been paid to do, for Tom had almost instinctively tried to protect the Rio Pintos Stagecoach Company's passengers and cargo. Nor had he been able to prevent the gambler, Barclay Parker, from opening fire.

Why had Wilson pumped lead at everyone? And who the hell was behind that other gun that had opened up on them from up above?

Then it seemed clear. They had set him up. Wilson had just duped him into thinking that it would be just him and that no one would get hurt. Hank had just been the guy who would get the Concord to the right place at the right moment. It was now obvious to him that with another gunman waiting to pick off the passengers on top, they had no intention of just robbing the stage. They hadn't really cared how many people got hurt.

He found himself pounding the bed with both fists. Well he would get him and whoever his murdering partner was. But first, he needed to know how many had survived the ambush, like him.

He pulled back the bedcovers, swung his legs over the side of the bed and stood up.

Then he felt himself go dizzy and light-headed. A moment later he had crashed to the floor. As he did so he had the momentary impression of the door opening and a woman gasping.

★   ★   ★

He found himself in bed again.

'You are making a habit of fainting,' came a man's voice. 'One of these times you won't have Miss Curtis to help you back to bed. Or me to tend to your cuts, bumps and bruises.'

Hank blinked his eyes open and found himself being watched by two people from the side of the bed; a man and a woman.

'I am Doctor Henry Johnson,' said the white-haired man in a well-worn black suit, as he wound the tubes of a stethoscope into a bundle, preparatory to stowing them away in a black medical bag. 'This is my house,' he explained, 'and Miss Curtis here has been your nurse for the past two days, ever since she got to Hastings Fork.'

'I am obliged to you both,' Hank replied, his eyes falling on Helen Curtis. He saw her cheeks suddenly go pink and he looked away.

'I am sorry, I didn't mean to stare, ma'am,' he said apologetically. 'It is just that . . . that I seem to have seen your face before.'

Helen Curtis was a beauty, with corn-yellow hair, sapphire-blue eyes and a peaches-and-cream complexion. She gave him a wan smile. 'No, we have never met, Mr Hawkins, I can assure you of that. But you have been drifting in and out of consciousness these past two days. You have seen me then.'

'Are you Tom Burton's fiancée?'

She blushed. 'Tom and I had been very close, but he had not asked me to marry him,' she replied. 'I believe he was going to ask me soon, but now . . . He never will. You may not know this, but Tom is dead, Mr Hawkins. He died in the ambush along with all the others.'

Hank stared back in horror as her eyes welled up with tears. 'All of them are dead?'

He shook his head in disbelief, then added: 'I am so sorry about Tom.'

Doctor Johnson laid a hand on his shoulder. 'This is all bound to be a shock to you, my boy. I am afraid that you are the only survivor. Sheriff Tyson has been waiting for you to recover enough in order to question you about what happened.'

He pointed to Hank's head. 'You had a head wound. It bled profusely, which is probably why the robbers didn't put another bullet in you. Fortunately, it just creased your scalp. I had to trim away some dead tissue and stitch it up, but it will heal up OK. I would just like you to keep a bandage on it for a couple of days longer. I'll change that one later.'

'I will, Doc, thank you. And the sheriff wants to talk to me, you say.'

'And so does Hiram Charlesworth,' added Helen.

'Hiram Charlesworth, the owner of the Rio Pintos Stagecoach Company, is here himself? In Hastings Fork?'

'The whole town is anxious to know what happened, Mr Hawkins,' the doctor went on. 'Lester Darton, the manager of the Hastings Fork branch of the Hagsworth Bank, keeled over and died when the news came in about the hold-up and the loss of the strongbox. He had a heart attack when he heard about it and died right where he fell. He has left a young widow. Those robbers have a hell of a lot to answer for.'

Hank felt a lump form in his throat and an almost overwhelming sense of guilt.

He reckoned that he had two choices. Either he could go to the sheriff and confess his part in the whole thing, which would be tantamount to saying that he was an accessory to the murders. Or he could get out of the bed and do whatever he needed to do to find Wilson and his murdering sidekick and bring them to justice. He knew that would mean incriminating himself and would inevitably put his own neck in a noose.

It was not an enviable choice, but the way he was feeling, it was the only thing to do. His greed had caused all those deaths. It was his desire to get enough money to buy a small spread of his own and raise cattle. But the price had been too high and now he figured he deserved to die.

'In that case, I thank you both for your care and I'll settle up with your fees before I leave Hastings Fork, but now I had better get going. I'll go see the sheriff first.'

He pointed at the pile of clothes, then looked up at Helen: 'I would appreciate it if you would excuse me while I dress.'

'If you are sure you feel strong enough to get up,' she said, then left the room.

Hank once again pulled back the covers and got out of bed. Doctor Johnson stood close in case he wobbled. This time he didn't fall.

'I am going to start my morning surgery now,' Doctor Johnson said. 'I'll want to check that head wound later today.'

He opened a door, which opened into his waiting room, which was already full of patients. Helen was sitting by the door. She stood up when he came through.

'I am coming with you to see the sheriff,' she said.

'Miss Curtis, I thank you for all that you have done, but — ' he began.

' — but nothing,' she replied. 'You have only just gotten out of bed after two days and you have fainted once already. Besides, I still don't know exactly how Tom died and I need to know. And please, call me Helen, rather than Miss Curtis.'

Hank looked down at her for a moment and then nodded. He knew that he had no option but to let her accompany him to the sheriff's office. 'Of course, Helen,' he said as he opened the door for her and they stepped outside on to the boardwalk.

He gingerly put on his Stetson over his bandaged head and winced in the process.

'Oh, that must still hurt, Mr Hawkins.'

He smiled thinly. 'Please, let's be equal about this. My name is Hank.'

As they walked along the boardwalk he wondered how she would feel about using his first name if she knew that his actions had led to Tom's death.

3

Hastings Fork was much like any other south-western town. It was a sprawling settlement made up of a mixture of clapboard wood-framed buildings and white-walled adobe fronts. There were one, two and three-storied buildings, four saloons and the usual assembly of various businesses and houses.

The sheriff's office was right at the end of Main Street, on the junction with Washington Street, which led to the respectable end of town where the peaceable folks lived. It was the part of town where the church and the church hall took pride of place. On the opposite side of the street, Lexington Street led to a warren of side alleys and dubious buildings where more nefarious activities and the town's less savoury folks lived and made a living. The nearest thing to a church there was Ebenezer Hood's Carpentry and Funeral Parlour.

Sheriff Cole Tyson had been the lawman in Hastings Fork for ten years. He was a tall, sandy-haired man with a drooping moustache and a slight hangdog expression that came about from his work, dealing as he did with those given to drink, violence and dishonest living. He was not a man given to patience, as evidenced by the justice that he gave out to malefactors with his fists and on occasion, with his twin Navy Colts.

Hank knocked on the office door and opened it, allowing Helen to precede him.

Cole Tyson was cleaning his guns at his desk. He wiped his hands on an oily rag and stood up.

'Miss Curtis,' he said with his usual slow drawl. 'And it's Hank Hawkins the driver, isn't it? Boy, I have been waiting to talk to you for a couple of days, because the trail of that gang has gone cold.'

'What gang, sheriff? How do you know it was a gang?'

The sheriff frowned. 'As a matter of fact, I don't know diddly-squat about what happened, except that when your stage didn't show up, me and my deputy, Danny Price, went to the Devil's Bones and found the stage stuck at the Devil's Knee. There were a number of boulders that had been rolled across the trail to stop it moving forward. The horses were screaming and snorting away and it's a wonder they hadn't pulled the Concord over the side. And we found six dead men and you, lying on the ground on a pool of blood.'

He sighed. 'Of course, everyone had been robbed and the strongbox had been busted loose from the rear boot and taken away. It was a dry gulch!'

Helen bit her lip. 'What does dry gulch mean, Sheriff Tyson?'

The lawman shook his head, his hangdog expression becoming even more doleful than usual. 'It means they aimed to kill everyone and rob them.'

The enormity of it all made Hank feel slightly nauseous again and he sat down and clutched the arms of the chair until the feeling passed. Then it dawned on him that something was not right.

'You found how many dead bodies?' Hank asked, suddenly.

'Six, including Tom Burton, Miss Curtis's young man. I think I've identified the others. After we had brought the Concord to town I sent my deputy to the swing station back along the trail. Abe Purcell gave us the best descriptions of the passengers that he could. We found names on various articles of luggage, papers and books.'

'How many passengers did he say he saw?'

'Five, plus young Tom Burton the messenger, and yourself. That accounts for six dead bodies. You're lucky you weren't the seventh.' Then his eyes narrowed and he asked: 'Why are you looking so surprised?'

'Old Abe Purcell the hostler has been

at the swing station for about twenty years, and he's a great man with horses, but I'm not so sure he is too hot with people. There were six passengers on the Concord.'

The sheriff looked shocked. 'You sure? Because if you are I hate to think that someone might have fallen into that ravine. Worse, I hate to think that they could still be alive and injured somewhere in the Devil's Bones. I'll send Danny Price out there right away to check the place over.'

He disappeared for a few moments to give instructions to his deputy in some back part of the building, then he returned and pointed to a coffee pot atop the potbelly stove in the corner.

'Now how about we all sit down and you tell us exactly what happened at the Devil's Knee.'

*   *   *

Hank had already thought about what he was going to say and had decided to say nothing about knowing Wilson, or that he had any knowledge about the robbery ahead of the event.

He described what happened to the best of his recollection, including the fact that he thought there were two gunmen involved. He described the duster coat and bandanna that Wilson was wearing, but admitted that he had been unable to see the other.

'Tom was a hero, Helen,' he said. 'He didn't flinch in the face of that armed gunman. He did his best to protect all of us.'

Helen Curtis had not touched her coffee, but had sat throughout it all tugging at a handkerchief in her lap. Her eyes had filled up with tears, but she had not broken down or cried.

'Did, did he suffer much?'

Hank laid a comforting hand on hers. 'It was instantaneous, Helen.'

She dabbed her eyes with the handkerchief and then leaned forward and took a sip of coffee. Then she stood up.

'That is what I have been waiting to hear, Hank. It is a relief to know that he behaved so bravely and that at least he didn't suffer an agonizing death. I think I'll go and lie down for a while. I'll see you at Doctor Johnson's house later, won't I?'

'Of course,' he said, standing up and opening the door for her. 'He wants to check my head. I have a few things that I need to do and then I'll be coming back.'

Once she had gone he talked with the sheriff for a while, really to reassure himself that the lawman had no suspicion of his having had any involvement in the whole evil business.

'Where are the bodies?' he asked. 'I expect that the funerals will be taking place soon.'

The sheriff frowned. 'Tom Burton's is this afternoon, because he had no family. Miss Curtis identified his body and so we can go ahead with it. It's all very difficult. There was no identifying information for one of them, so I haven't been able to notify next of kin. The families of three others have been contacted and they are on their way. And there is another that I'm having difficulty contacting friends.' He waved a hand in front of his face. 'But you are right, in this heat they'll have to be buried soon.'

Hank brushed invisible dust off his Stetson and clicked his tongue. 'It is a dirty business, sheriff, and one that I am determined to help resolve. I reckon I will try and pick up the trail on these devils.'

'Well, you are a private individual and I can't stop you from doing that, but you be careful. Those men are vicious killers and if you somehow found them, which I doubt you can do, since there are no obvious trails to follow, then you have a good chance of ending up dead.'

Hank nodded. 'I appreciate that, sheriff, but I need to try.'

Cole Tyson could see the determination in his eyes and imagined that he would feel the same if he had been the sole survivor of a dry gulching.

'Mind if I take a look at the bodies?' Hank asked. 'I feel that I need to pay my respects, what with them being passengers on the stage I was driving. And I ought to be able to put names to them all. At least, the names they were using.'

'Feel free, my friend. Feel free,' said the sheriff. 'And I'd appreciate you leaving their names. Either with me or with the undertaker.'

Hank nodded and put on his Stetson as he made for the door. Feeling free was something he thought he would never feel again. He did not think he could ever be free of the guilt that seemed to be gnawing away at him that moment.

* * *

Ebenezer Hood was a wizened man of about sixty, stick-thin and with a small goatee beard, but without an accompanying moustache. He was working in his carpentry, building a coffin. He was wearing a collarless work shirt with his sleeves rolled up, and his trademark top hat.

Hank introduced himself and explained the reason for his visit.

The undertaker nodded and held out a hand. 'I am glad that at least one of you poor souls made it,' he said. 'I had to prettify some of the bodies; they had so many bullet wounds. At least Tom Burton's only had a chest wound; they spared his face. His girl, Helen Curtis didn't have to see his handsome features all ruined.'

He lay down a wood plane and gestured for Hank to follow him. He went through a back door and then through another door into his funeral parlour. First of all he went into a room whose only light source was a small stained glass window. On a table stood a wooden cross and in the middle of the room was an open coffin supported on a large trestle table.

'He's still in my chapel of rest,' he

said, signalling for Hank to have a look at the body. 'He's all ready for his funeral this afternoon.'

Hank felt a mix of emotions course through him. There was anger and fury that the young man's life had been snuffed out when he had such a bright future to look forward to with Helen. It was followed by profound sadness at the loss of a good friend. But most intense of all was a surge of guilt that made him want to sigh.

Tears formed in his eyes, but he did not feel that he could allow any emotions to show in front of the undertaker. He stood with his Stetson in his hand and mumbled a farewell to Tom.

'Two of the others are in my embalming room and the other three are out in my back room, already in their coffins.'

Hank followed into the embalming room where two bodies were lying on two tables specially fitted with guttering around the edges. On side tables were bottles and the assorted instruments of the undertaker's art. The air was acrid and made Hank's eyes water and his throat feel tight.

'That's the latest embalming fluid,' Ebenezer Hood explained. 'It's called formaldehyde. My funeral parlour is probably about the first in this neck of the woods to use it.'

Hank held his breath and looked down at the fully clad bodies of the whiskey drummer and of the French chef, Gaston Legrand. The whiskey drummer, whose name he did not know, was wearing his hat, which Ebenezer had cut away at that back so that it could look normal with him lying on his back.

'I've been experimenting with how he'll look,' he explained. 'Half his head was blown away and his wife is coming out for his funeral. I figured a hat was the only way to make him look respectable for her to see.'

He pointed to the French chef, although Hank suspected that he had merely trained in France and taken a French name to sound more professional. 'Monsoor Legrand,' he said, boldly trying to say it with a French accent, 'had two chest wounds, so he's been easy to prepare. I'll get them coffined up as soon as I finish their boxes.'

They went through to the back room where three closed coffins lay in a row on the floor. 'I'm running out of space. If anyone else dies today I'll be stacking them up. It's a good thing that we had Lester Darton's funeral yesterday.'

Without more ado he lifted the lid on the first coffin.

Hank nodded. 'That's O'Leary. Don't know his first name, but he was a miner.'

'The sheriff will be pleased to know a name, even if it is just the one. I'm going to have to embalm him soon, in case he's going to be a while before we plant him.'

Hank waited for him to replace the lid and open the next.

He nodded as he recognized the

gambler. 'That is Barclay Parker. He was a professional gambling man. Poor guy, he took one gamble too many by drawing on that gunman.'

'Whoever shot him made pretty sure. He had one shot in the upper chest, a belly shot and one in the heart.'

He lowered the lid and moved to the last one. 'And this is another that is giving the sheriff a headache. We know who he is, but we can't read the name of the Church or the town in his bible.'

'Ah, the Reverend Eli Tabner,' said Hank with a nod. 'Did they spoil his features?'

'See for yourself,' replied Ebenezer Hood as he prised off the lid.

Hank stared in disbelief at the body of a man wearing a preacher's shirt and a clerical collar. The undertaker had placed the wire-framed spectacles on his nose and placed the bible in his hands over his chest.

But it wasn't the body of Eli Tabner, the preacher. It was the wrangler he had known as Dusty.

4

Hank had not intimated to the undertaker that the man in the coffin was not the Reverend Eli Tabner. Indeed, he doubted now whether there actually was any such person at all.

Damn them! he thought, as he made his way back to the sheriff's office. His temper was rising; for it was clear to him now that he had been totally duped and that the man who had pretended to be a preacher was part of the gang. And now he knew that they actually were a gang consisting of at least three people, since there had been someone shooting at them from the top of the canyon wall. He presumed that had it proved necessary, the preacher would have shot them from behind.

He wondered whether he ought to tell Sheriff Tyson. Part of him thought that would be the responsible thing to do, to help the law. But a voice inside him said that would merely delay him in his purpose. Come hell or high water, he was going to find them and make them pay, or die in the trying.

'I recognized the big guy,' he told the sheriff. 'His name was O'Leary and he was a miner. He was Irish, if that is any help.'

'It's a start, but I can't think it will help a lot, not unless someone comes looking for him. He'll probably just end up in Boot Hill with a board tacked to a cross saying 'Someone O'Leary — victim of a Dry Gulch gang'.'

That added fuel to Hank's sense of anger and guilt. It shouldn't be the way that someone's life should end. Snuffed out by greed.

He stopped off at the gunsmith's shop a couple of businesses down from the sheriff's office and after some hefting, balancing and prevaricating, bought himself a Peacemaker, gunbelt and holster and an 1873 Winchester carbine, with a supply of .44–40 cartridges that would fit both weapons. He paid from the wad of money that he habitually kept in his right boot and which the dry gulch robbers had not found.

It was ironic, he thought, since the bulk of that wad had been a prepayment from Wilson when he agreed to stop the stage at the Devil's Knee.

It had been a while since he had carried guns, although for several years he had never been without one, for he had served as a town marshal down on the Panhandle. He had given them up and sworn never to use them again on the night that a drunken cowboy, probably no more than eighteen years old, had killed Burt Kincaid, his deputy who had gone to arrest him. When Hank had shown up the kid had panicked and threw lead at him, killing a local shopkeeper and wounding a saloon girl. Hank had shot him in the belly.

It took two days before the kid died.

And now, he was about to break his promise. He felt it wouldn't matter much, considering the weight of guilt that he felt for the deaths of Tom Burton and the passengers of the Concord.

* ★ ★

He hadn't realized how hungry he was until he returned to Doc Johnson's surgery.

The smell of apple pie mingled with that of fresh coffee made his stomach go into spasms. He let himself into the doc's private quarters by the door at the end of the waiting room.

Helen Curtis was in the kitchen talking with someone. Hank knocked on the door and went in.

Her gaze fell on the Peacemaker and the Winchester carbine in his hand. He thought he detected a look of concern flash across her face. Then she gestured towards the man who turned in his chair.

'There's someone to see you, Hank,' she said.

Hank immediately recognized Hiram Charlesworth, the Rio Pintos Stage-coach Company owner, for he had worked for him for three years. He was a man in his mid-forties, clean-shaven, with wiry black hair, going silver at the temples. He had an affable smile and was known for taking good care of his employees.

'My dear Hank,' said the stagecoach owner, rising to his feet and holding out his hand. 'I cannot tell you how relieved I am that you have recovered. We have been most concerned about you. Come and sit down and have a coffee.'

Hank laid his Winchester in the corner and took a seat.

Helen poured him a cup of coffee and cut him a large slice of apple pie.

'Will that do?' she asked. 'I can fix you some bacon and eggs if you want, but after what you have been through, not eating for two days, I thought this would be gentle of your stomach. And there is plenty more, if you can manage it.'

Hank thanked her and tucked in with the spoon she had placed in front of him.

Hiram Charlesworth sat patiently and politely while he ate. Then once Hank pushed his plate aside with a satisfied sigh he leaned forward.

'Miss Curtis has told me what you remember about the robbery. I don't mind telling you, this is the worst thing that has ever happened to my company. It is tragic. Poor Tom Burton.'

'Are you coming to his funeral this afternoon?' Helen asked Hank.

'Of course,' he replied. 'I wouldn't miss it for the world.' He shook his head. 'But then I am afraid that I need to go.'

'Go where?' Hiram asked. 'You know I don't expect you to come back to work for a week, or even two.'

Hank turned to his employer. 'That's just it, Mr Charlesworth. I reckon I need to quit. I have something to do and I need to leave as soon as possible.'

'You didn't answer my question,

Hank. Go where?'

'After those murdering dogs.'

A slow smile spread across the stagecoach owner's face. 'You have spirit, Hank, I'll say that. But don't go dashing off straight after the funeral. I want to have a word with you.' He stood up. 'Helen, I thank you for the coffee. Can you tell the doctor I'll see him later? Right now I have to pay a visit to Laura Darton. She's distraught after Lester's sudden death and I kind of feel a responsibility to her, on account of the fact that my Concord was carrying the bank's money.' He shook his head. 'I was there when he died. It was horrible.'

There was an awkward pause. With so many deaths, saying sorry just didn't seem adequate.

'I'll see you then, Mr Charlesworth,' Hank said, as he nodded acceptance of Helen's offer to refill his coffee cup.

'Do, do you really plan to go after them?' she asked, once Hiram had gone.

'I do.'

'But how will you find them?'

'I have some experience in tracking, Helen,' he replied as he lifted his coffee to his lips.

What he didn't tell her was that he had talked with one of the gang when he arranged his part in it. He planned to start right there.

★   ★   ★

Tom Burton's funeral was well attended, despite the fact that he did not live in Hastings Fork. Perhaps it was the manner of his death, or that he was seen as someone who had done his best to defend the passengers and the stage-coach company's cargo against armed robbers. Whatever the reason, the townsfolk turned out to pay their respects at the tiny church, and then at the graveside.

Hank noticed that Hiram his boss was there, standing with a woman dressed in black, with a black toque and veil. He presumed she was Laura Darton, the bank manager's widow. He could see that she was sobbing. The poor woman, he thought.

Helen was also dressed in a black dress, but without hat or veil. She hung her head and tears glistened in her eyes, but she held her resolve and stood firm, with her bible clasped in one hand and a single rose in the other.

The Reverend Boorman, an elderly man with thin white hair conducted the service in a dull, melancholic manner.

'So let us commend our brother to the Lord, that the Lord may embrace him in peace and raise up his body on the last day. Amen.'

Helen tossed the rose on to the coffin and stood for a few moments, then bowed her head and blew a kiss to the grave before turning to be escorted away from the grave by the priest.

Hank had been standing at the back of the crowd of mourners, mainly because he felt his presence too near to Tom's grave would be something of an affront. It was also because he felt too guilty to be close to the man whose death he had been instrumental in causing.

Sheriff Tyson was waiting at the wrought iron cemetery gate. 'My deputy had a good scout around the Devil's Knee and along the trail, but didn't find any trace of another body. It's mighty peculiar. Are you sure there was another passenger? Old Abe Purcell at the swing station could only account for five passengers, plus Tom Burton and you.'

Hank was anxious to be gone. He clicked his tongue and ran a hand across the stubble on his chin. 'To be honest, Sheriff Tyson, I'm not sure at all now. Maybe it was the knock on my head. Maybe I just thought I'd seen another person.'

The sheriff nodded. 'That's pretty much what I reckoned.' He nodded at the Peacemaker in the holster hanging against Hank's right thigh. 'Judging by that gun and the Winchester carbine, you intend on having a reckoning with that gang.'

'I surely do.'

'Well, like I said, be careful. But I doubt if you'll have much success. Me and my deputy couldn't pick up any trail in that canyon. And once they were out of it, heck, they could just disappear into the Pintos.'

'Maybe I just feel more motivated than you, sheriff.'

The lawman stared back at him with narrowed eyes. 'No-one has questioned my motivation before, mister.'

Hank tipped his Stetson to him. 'I wasn't implying there was anything wrong with it, sheriff. Now if you'll excuse me, I figure I need to get my things ready and arrange for a horse.'

As he made his way to the livery stable to buy a horse he thought he felt the lawman's eyes staring at his back. He knew that he should have held out and assured the sheriff that there were six passengers, rather than five, but that might have delayed him further.

He also had not wanted to explain that his motivation was not just about justice, it was about seeking revenge and with the Lord's blessing, assuaging some of the guilt he felt.

★   ★   ★

If there was one thing that Hank knew about, it was horses. The livery owner had been willing to sell him a horse, but not the one that Hank wanted. He wanted a paint that he just knew after running his hands over it and getting to know it that it would have stamina and a turn of speed if necessary.

He was negotiating when Hiram Charlesworth came into the barn.

'I'll buy that horse for you, Hank,' he said, holding an unlit cigar between his teeth.

'Why would you offer that, Mr Charlesworth?'

'Because I want to make a deal with you.'

'Go on.'

'Catch those killers and bring them back to justice and I'll give you the same reward that Sheriff Tyson is going to put up.'

'I didn't know he had put up any wanted posters.'

'He's about to. Five hundred dollars for each of the two gunmen. I saw the sheriff and he said you told him there were two of them.'

'That's right, I told him that,' Hank admitted. He saw no reason to tell his boss that there was a third, who had masqueraded as a passenger.

'Well, you bring them in, dead or alive, like he's going to put on his posters, and you'll get one thousand dollars from him and I'll give you another thousand.' He looked slightly bashful. 'And if you can bring back the money they stole from the bank, I'm sure that the Hagsworth Bank would pay a reward. I think I could see to that.'

Hank shook his head. 'Money isn't

really the reason that I am going after them.'

'I understand that. You feel outraged that they committed this dreadful crime and that they killed your friend, Tom Burton. But to show my good will and faith in you, I want to give you this horse and five hundred dollars fee, whether you catch them or not.'

Hank looked warily at him. 'Now why would you do that? I am going anyway.'

'Because I want you to take someone with you.'

Hank shook his head. 'I am riding alone.'

Henry Masterson, the bow-legged livery owner, had been standing with his arms crossed, chewing on the stem of an old corncob pipe. 'Are you buying this horse or not? I'll take fifty dollars for it.'

'Done,' said Hiram, peeling off bills from a wad, without even bothering to haggle for it. 'So if you could just let me have a bill of sale, Henry.'

While the old man went off to prepare the receipt Hiram peeled off five hundred dollars and held it towards Hank.

'I haven't agreed.'

There was the sound of someone else coming into the livery behind them.

'Ah, here is your companion on this quest,' said Hiram.

Hank turned and his eyes widened in amazement. It was Helen Curtis and she had dressed in range clothes, having tucked her hair into a hat that he recognized as having belonged to Tom Burton.

'You are kidding me?' he gasped. 'I couldn't possibly take Helen. I can't expose her to danger like that.'

'I see you haven't told him, Mr Charlesworth,' she said.

'I was just about to get his agreement, Helen.'

'Well you haven't,' said Hank. 'It is not possible. I won't do it. I am riding alone.'

Henry Masterson reappeared with

the bill of sale. He handed it to Hiram Charlesworth, and then he beamed at Helen.

'I've got your horse all ready, whenever you want her,' he said to her.

'I'll need it at the same time as Hank needs his,' she replied with a tired smile. 'We'll be riding together.'

Hiram stuffed the wad of money in Hank's shirt pocket. 'It's all settled, Hank.'

'It is not!' Hank persisted.

Helen smiled at Hank. 'Oh but it is. You see, you can't stop me from riding where I want. And when you go, I go. Why on earth would you think that I wouldn't want to bring these men to justice?'

'But you . . . '

'But what? I am a woman? Well yes, I am, but I can also ride and I can shoot a Winchester — possibly even as well as you.'

Hiram patted his shoulder. 'Helen Curtis is a determined woman, Hank. And my guess is that she is more resourceful than you could ever imagine.'

Hank looked at her and despite himself, nodded his head. He couldn't help hearing Tom's words echoing in his mind. He had said she was a woman worth dying for. If things went badly wrong, he might just find that out for himself.

5

After buying a few items he thought he might need on the trip from Dunmore's Emporium, Hank had collected his meagre possessions and stowed them away in his saddle-bags.

They rode out of town together, retracing the trail that Hank had driven the Concord along a hundred times before. To begin with their conversation had been confined to that, as Helen asked him about his driving and about how well he had known Tom, and how he had become a stagecoach driver. He had not wanted to tell her about his life as a lawman, but she had a way about her that made him want to tell her the truth. Or at least, as much as he dared tell her. He was all too aware that the longer he withheld the truth from her, the harder it would be to rectify the situation.

So be it, he thought to himself. He was on a mission and her presence was simply an added complication. Whatever he did, he had to make sure that she came to no harm. He owed that much to Tom.

'And how long were you a lawman?'

'Five years, down on the Panhandle. It was a good job, but a tough life.'

'A violent life?'

He took a deep intake of breath, which gave away his feelings about it before he said anything. 'Yes, there was violence. Those trail towns get a lot of frustrated cowboys passing through them. And gamblers, tricksters and more than their share of people who drink too much and try to prove something.'

The images of Burt Kincaid, his deputy, lying dead in his coffin along with the 18-year-old kid who had shot him, a storekeeper and wounded one of the Four Kings dance girls haunted him most days. That had been good reason to give up the gun, until the massacre of

Tom and all those passengers at Devil's Knee had forced him to make a fresh promise: one that necessitated him bearing arms again.

'Did you know that Tom was talking about becoming a lawman?' Helen asked.

He turned in surprise. 'No, he never told me that.'

She smiled wanly. 'I suspect there was a lot that he hadn't told you. Like the fact that he admired you a lot. It was because you had been a lawman that he wanted to do the same thing.'

That jolted him inside. He had never realized that Tom had any such notion. Nor had he been aware that he thought of him as anything other than a competent stage driver.

'I am surprised at that, Helen. I don't think I told him too much about my lawman days.'

'He said that you were a modest man and that from bits and pieces that you told him, he had worked out the sort of man you were. He wanted to emulate you.'

'I am not the man he thought me to be,' Hank said truthfully. 'There are things about me that I am not proud of.'

'Everyone could say that, Hank.'

He shrugged and readjusted his position in his saddle. 'But how did you two meet?'

'After church one Sunday. We were having a church party and I was teaching some of the children how to paint.'

Hank thought about Tom's watch, with the tiny self-portrait that she had made for it.

'I hadn't realized that Tom was a churchgoer. I never saw him on a Sunday.'

'He lived his life according to Christian principles,' she said. 'He was a really fine young man and we . . . we became very close.'

Hank put his hand on the pommel of his saddle and turned. 'Helen, why exactly have you insisted on coming with me?'

'For the same reason that you are going, Hank. I want justice for Tom. I want the men who did that — what did Sheriff Tyson call it — that dry gulching, brought to trial.'

Hank shook his head. 'I am going to do my best to bring them to justice, Helen, but it just might not be possible to take them alive. I may have to shoot them to defend us.'

She stared back at him, her sapphire blue eyes fixed upon him. 'So be it.' She leaned forward and tapped the butt of her Winchester in its scabbard. 'If it comes to shooting I am ready and I am even willing to die.' Her eyes misted with tears.

'I loved Tom, you see. I loved him with all my heart.' Her voice trembled. 'He . . . he was worth dying for.'

⋆　⋆　⋆

The trail began weaving in and out of boulders and red stacks interspersed with scrub oak and various types of vegetation before reaching the huge red walls of the Pintos. There the trail ducked downwards and they rode into the network of canyons known as the Devil's Bones.

The noise of the horses' hoofs echoed eerily around the canyon walls.

'This is called the Devil's Elbow,' Hank said as they rode along a ledge that doubled back sharply upon itself. 'There is plenty of room for us, but if you imagine a Concord trundling along here pulled by six horses then you'll get an idea of how easy it would be to hold one up.'

Ten minutes later they were moving along the ledge of the Devil's Knee itself.

Helen winced at the sight of the chasm that fell away to the side.

'It took place up ahead,' Hank said, pointing. 'But if you don't mind, just wait here and let me have a look around. That spot over there, on the edge of the ravine is where the gunman started shooting.'

He dismounted and made his way to where the man he knew as Wilson had held them up and fired his first shot, the one that had killed Tom. Then he had taken a couple of steps sideward to the edge and started firing into the Concord, killing first the whiskey drummer and then Barclay Parker and Gaston Legrand.

He wasn't at all sure that he could even determine footprints amid the churned up dust where the six horses and the Concord had been driven after Sheriff Tyson and his deputy had recovered it. He saw the boulders that had been rolled to the canyon wall and which had been used to prevent the horses moving forward.

He dropped to his knees and surveyed the ground. In part, he felt he needed to make it seem to Helen that he was looking for clues.

'Have you found anything?' she called out.

'I think so. I am just building the scene up in my mind.'

He stood then walked forward, examining the ground where the horses had stood screaming and pounding the ground in their terror. It must have been dreadful for them, he thought.

It was dreadful for him to relive it as well. He pictured the exact position of the Concord and imagined all of the passengers and himself. As he did so he could imagine the shooter from up above on the canyon rim throwing lead down at them. He recalled hearing rather than seeing two shots and then he saw the Irishman O'Leary being thrown forward with two shots in his back. It was then that he reached for Tom's shotgun in an attempt to blast Wilson, the first gunman. There was more gunfire and screams and then he was hit before he could get a shot off.

In his mind's eye he saw himself pitching forward to land on the ground. He had no recollection beyond that, but he knew that he was lucky not to have broken his neck or other bones in that fall. The blood from his head wound and the height he had tumbled from must have convinced Wilson and his confederate that he was dead.

He examined the ground where he would have fallen and saw the staining where the blood had soaked the earth.

'But who killed Dusty?' he mused.

'Who killed who?' came Helen's voice from close behind him.

He spun round, his gun appearing in his hand. He saw that she had dismounted, tethered the horses and advanced quietly alongside the canyon wall.

'I didn't hear you, Helen,' he said apologetically, returning his gun to its holster. 'I should have warned you, it's best not creep up on me in this situation. From this moment on I am going to be on my alert, which means my hand may never be far from my gun.'

Helen had looked startled at the sight and speed with which the gun had appeared in Hank's hand. She regained her cool instantly.

'Who killed who?' she repeated.

'I was just trying to build the picture of the whole dry gulching in my head. When I was shot I heard more gunfire, but I am not sure where it came from. There were two men behind me. One was a wrangler called Dusty and the other was a preacher who called himself Eli Tabner.'

'You said that there was a body missing when we were in the sheriff's office, didn't you? The sheriff was going to send his deputy to check it out.'

'Which he did, but he didn't find any body,' Hank explained. He frowned. 'I should have told the sheriff, but I was worried that he was going to delay me. There definitely was another person, but the reason that they didn't find another body is because he isn't dead.'

'I don't understand.'

'The man dressed up as a preacher was one of them, Helen. It was either him or the guy shooting from the canyon rim that killed Dusty the wrangler.'

'So they really are a gang, not just two men.'

'There are three of them. But there is more. The preacher swapped clothes with Dusty. I presume to make everyone think that he is dead.'

Helen blew air through her lips. 'These are devious and evil men. So what now?'

Hank pointed to the canyon rim. 'I need to get up there and see if the third man left any clues behind.'

★　★　★

It took some time to find a way of ascending the canyon wall, then a good twenty minutes for Hank to climb. At last he pulled himself over the edge and lay for a moment gathering his breath, for it took more out of him than he thought it would and he felt slightly dizzy.

He waved down to Helen who had returned to the horses.

'Now let's see if you have left any

calling cards,' he whispered to himself as he made his way along the rim to the point where he estimated the shooter had fired from.

He found an area of flattened vegetation. Getting down on his hands he scrutinized it. Within moments he had found the stubs of three cheroots and three .44–40 cartridges. It seemed likely that the shooter had used a Winchester on O'Leary and possibly also on Dusty. That would mean that either Wilson had been the one who had shot him or this man. Or then again, it could have been the preacher. Who knows what sort of weapon he had on him.

But if it had been the preacher, then how could he have missed Hank at that range?

And would Wilson have fired if the preacher, his man had been so close to Hank. It didn't make a whole lot of sense.

As he thought about it he looked at the three cigar stubs and thought that they looked slightly odd. None of them had toothmarks on them, as was often the case when men chewed the end. Not only that, but each had a tiny hole in the side, as if they had been pricked with a match or something. Maybe it was to let air in, he wondered. Then with a shrug, he pocketed one of them along with the three cartridges.

He stood up and waved to Helen to let her know that he was on his way down. He steeled himself, for he knew that he would have to seem confident when he got down.

'We have to go deep into the Pintos,' he told her some twenty minutes later when he had completed his descent without mishap. 'I found some cheroot stubs and some cartridges. Three of each. That means that the shooter up there had been waiting some considerable time. I saw where he had climbed up and then went down again. I am pretty sure that those cheroots came from a trading post that services a lot of the silver miners.'

'Is it far?'

'About an hour, but first of all we need to get to a stream.'

'Are you thirsty?' she asked. 'I have plenty water in my canteen.'

He shook his head with a smile. 'No, we just have some things to do before we go to the trading post.'

Helen did not press matters. They mounted their horses and she followed him back along the way that they had come for about a mile, then they took another trail that led off into one of the other canyons.

When they came to the stream that he mentioned they made a temporary camp and he set a fire and brewed some coffee.

'Aren't you worried about smoke?'

'No, we're safe here. I don't think they will be within miles of here. In fact, I doubt if they are at all concerned. They will have thought that they killed everyone and that they left no clues for anyone to follow.'

'Except for a smart tracker, like you,'

she said with the ghost of a smile.

'I am not so smart,' he replied.

He opened one of his saddle-bags and pulled out a rough jacket and a wide-brimmed shapeless hat.

'These are for you.'

'Why?'

'Because where we are going and the sort of men that we might meet I don't want anyone getting ideas. You will excuse me for saying so, Helen, but you are too good-looking. From now on you are my little brother and these clothes should make you look like that. Stick your hair well up inside the hat. Put Tom's hat in your saddle-bag.'

She did as he bid and then stood with her arms held out from her sides. 'Will I do? Am I boyish enough for you now?'

He nodded.

'And now, I have to change how I look.' He unwound the bandage from his head and produced a pair of scissors and a bottle from the other saddle-bag. 'If you wouldn't mind chopping off most of my hair, then I'm going to bleach it and turn it blond. That's why I need the stream.'

Ten minutes later, clean-shaven, with short hair and eyebrows all dyed blond and sporting a pair of wire-framed spectacles, Hank looked totally different. He completed the transformation by donning a different shirt, jacket and an equally misshapen hat as hers. Reluctantly he stowed his own Stetson in his saddle-bag.

'I reckon I could be a schoolteacher and you are my little brother. We're aiming to try our luck mining and see if we can make our fortunes.'

'You do realize that I am a schoolteacher. Why can't I be the teacher and you can be my dumb big brother?'

Despite himself he grinned. 'Not looking like that, you can't.'

And to his surprise they both found themselves laughing at the joke.

It was the first time that he had not felt quite so tense in her company.

6

It took them a little over an hour to make their way through the rest of the Devil's Bones canyon system. Then the land became more undulating and the vegetation became more scrub-like, interspersed with various types of cactus.

Here and there they saw evidence of old mines in the hills that had either played out or which had failed to yield much ore at all.

'You'll find that folks often climb higher and start their mines in places where they are least likely to be spied upon, or worse, robbed,' Hank explained. 'The miners are a pretty tough type of guys, willing to put up with any kind of hardship. It isn't easy living away out here on your own, neither looking for nor welcoming other people at your mine.'

'And so do you think that we will

look like aspiring miners?' she asked with a smile.

'We better hope so. One thing for sure, we don't look like the same people who entered the Devil's Bones. We have a sort of greenhorn look about us, which should help. If folks think we are kind of green, then they won't perceive us as any kind of threat.'

He pointed at her Winchester. 'Can you really use that gun?'

With the slightest raise of an eyebrow she pulled it out of her scabbard, levered a bullet in and swiftly took aim at the forked branch of a scrub oak some fifty yards off. It shattered and the wood fell to the ground.

'Is that good enough, Hank? My father used to take me hunting when I was a little girl and he taught me to shoot most types of gun. This Winchester just about aims and fires itself.'

'I am impressed. But I think that we ought to use different names. How about me being Leroy and you . . . '

'I'll be Billy. I'm seventeen years old

and I sure want to help my big brother work a mine. We're going to send money back east to our elderly folks.'

'You've given it some thought, I see.'

'That's what I do, Leroy. I think, just the way you've been trying to get me to do. Logically and without getting in a fluster. I do surely thank you for giving me such a good grounding in algebra.'

'I can see that you have the ways of a teacher with you, Helen.'

'You mean Billy,' she corrected, as she slid the Winchester back into the scabbard.

Hank nodded and rode on.

★   ★   ★

Macgregor's Trading Post was a sprawling two-storeyed timber building with a well-stocked coral, hitching posts, an outside privy some fifty feet from it and piles of barrels, crates and tins along one outer wall.

'The story goes that old man Macgregor is a Scotsman who came here thirty years ago, made a reasonable amount of money mining, but found out he made more by trading. He's been here ever since, providing miners with supplies, horses, burros and whatever equipment they might need. They trade silver and everyone is happy.'

'I smell cooking,' said Helen.

'Yes, he cooks, serves bar and is partial to a bit of gambling, although to hear him talk you would think he never plays poker himself. People come from miles around to enjoy his facilities. Let's amble in for some food and drink. Just let me do all the talking. You are shy, remember that.'

'Yes, Leroy,' she returned. Then, catching his arm she asked, 'Are you sure he won't recognize you?'

He shook his head and gave her what he thought was a confident smile. In truth, he hoped rather than thought Macgregor would not remember him. Although he wanted more than anything to catch up with Wilson, he definitely didn't want Macgregor to mention that he had been there recently and had seemed to be in deep discussion with a man.

They hitched their horses, mounted the stoop leading up to a porch that was covered in a rough, but undoubtedly welcome awning. A couple of grizzled old miners were sitting, smoking pipes and drinking beer.

'Sure, it is hot as hell today,' one of them said with an unmistakable Irish brogue. 'I recommend you have one of Macgregor's beers.'

'Or better still, three of his beers,' the other said with a wheezy laugh.

'That's if you can afford his prices. The only trading post this part of the Pintos and he knows how to charge.'

'We don't drink alcohol,' Hank replied as he adjusted his spectacles and headed past them. 'Come on, Billy.'

Inside, the air hung thick with a pall of tobacco smoke. As their eyes became accustomed to the hazy light that shone through several greasy and fly-stained windows they saw that the place was really quite crowded. There were men leaning at a long bar drinking whiskey or beer. There were groups sitting at two tables playing poker and at another playing chuck-a-luck, a game with a wicker birdcage containing dice. There was noise, the clink of money and the tinkle of glasses.

The far end of the hall was a sort of store, with racks of ropes, mining tools and heaps of assorted clothes. Beside that were sacks of flour, animal feed and tins of food. Then there were cases of guns, knives and, high atop a cupboard with a blackboard chalked out with the word DANGER, there were a couple of crates of dynamite. And dotted here and there were other tables at which men ate and drank, while a couple went rushing hither and thither taking orders and serving food.

'Welcome, gentlemen,' boomed out a voice from behind the bar. They looked round and saw a giant of a man; a six and a half foot tall, red-headed man with a full red beard. He was wearing a derby hat at a slight angle, an apron over a collarless shirt, with his sleeves rolled up to the elbows to reveal huge, ham-sized forearms. 'Come in, sit down or stand, whatever it is you need, you'll find it at Finlay Macgregor's Trading Post.'

Hank tipped his hat at him. 'That is kind of you sir,' he said, with what Helen noticed to be a slightly nasal and higher voice than he normally used. 'The name is Leroy Jones and this is my little brother Billy. We would appreciate some food and some drink. Would you happen to have any milk?'

The large Scotsman did not even flinch at their choice of drink, unlike some of his clientele, some of whom looked decidedly bleary-eyed. One snorted with derision at the thought of a man drinking milk for pleasure and returned to his own beer and whiskey.

'No problem at all! Macgregor caters for all tastes and I get fresh milk twice a week. Sit you down over in that far corner and I'll send a lad to take your orders and bring your milk.' He winked. 'It is not what you would call an extensive menu, but you have a choice. You don't have to have chillies in your stew.'

'And after we have eaten we would like to buy some equipment. We are heading into the hills to start a mine.'

Several heads flashed round at this news, but after a moment's appraisal most people seemed to lose interest in the two brothers. They had, Hank thought, assessed them as novices who would be wasting their time.

They threaded their way between the tables and found a vacant one at the far end of the hall, where before long a tousle-headed young man with an unfortunate crop of spots on his face came and took their order for milk and stew and beans. Hank chose his with chillies and Helen had hers without.

While they waited Hank pointed to a small counter atop which was a sign asserting the wonder of Bull Durham tobacco. Beside it were boxes of cigars and cheroots, and jars of different types of tobacco. In a basket there were a variety of corncob, clay and cherry-wood pipes.

'Those are the exact type of cheroots that the shootist was smoking,' he whispered. 'I'd be willing to bet on it.'

'But how likely are we to find him here?' she said softly.

But Hank didn't seem to have heard her. Instead, he was staring at a table close by. There were four men playing poker round it. Two were swarthy miners, one looked like a drifter and the last had the look of a gambling man.

Their food and milk arrived and both ate with gusto.

'What have you seen, big brother?' Helen asked at last, careful to keep her voice low.

'Take a look at that gambler over at that table. You'll see that he has a cheroot smoking away in the ashtray by his side.'

'So what is the significance of that?

You can't think it is him?'

'Watch him smoke it.'

And as Helen did so, the man, clean-shaven and smartly dressed with a thin moustache and two silver rings on each hand, picked up his cheroot. But he wasn't holding it in his hands. Instead he had lifted a silver toothpick, which had pierced the side of the cheroot. He raised it to his lips, puffed and then blew out a stream of blue smoke. He gingerly replaced the cheroot in the ashtray, then he laughed as he took his turn to reveal his hand of cards. Clearly he had won, since there was thumping on the table by the two miners and a curse from the drifter as the gambler reached forward and scooped the substantial pot of money towards himself.

'The man doesn't want to risk getting tar staining on his hands, I reckon,' said Hank. 'Unless I am mistaken, that is our man.'

* * *

After they had finished their meal Hank managed to get Finlay Macgregor's attention in order to buy some equipment.

Hank gave a good imitation of an innocent teacher to such an extent that Finlay Macgregor was able to sell him all that he needed and probably more.

'And you'll want some dynamite,' he said, reaching effortlessly up to one of the crates of dynamite and pulling out a couple of sticks. He smiled and held them out to Hank. 'Have you used this stuff before?' he asked doubtfully.

'I have seen it used and I understand the risks,' Hank replied.

'Best to keep the lad away from it,' Finlay added with a wink at Helen. 'With all due respect, that is. You see, more than one youngster has blown himself up by underestimating how powerful this stuff can be.'

'I'll watch my brother, sir,' Hank replied. 'He can be a bit slow in the uptake sometimes, but he is going to learn the mining business with me and make a fortune.'

'Well, there is surely plenty of silver up in the Pintos and if you work hard and have a measure of good luck, fortune may smile on you.' He tapped the side of his nose. 'You'll have a better chance of making a fortune than you will by playing poker.'

He looked down at Helen who had bent her head slightly to prevent him getting too good a sight of her. 'See that table over there. Well those two miners and the cowboy fellow are just handing over all their well-earned money to that gambling man. He's a real dude.'

'Does he come here often?' Hank asked. 'He doesn't look like a man that does much hard physical work.'

Finlay guffawed. 'He doesn't do a lot, I don't think. He calls himself Silver, on account of his silver rings and that silver toothpick that he uses to smoke his cigars as well as keep his teeth clean.'

A voice called from the bar and he

turned and waved at the thirsty customer. 'I'll be right with you,' he shouted. Then to Hank: 'Have you got a burro to carry all this stuff?'

'That was our next question.'

'I thought not. Give me five minutes then I'll help you out with your purchases and we'll sort out a burro.'

Once he had gone Hank drew Helen aside. 'We have to look the parts so a burro makes sense. I suggest that we also — '

Angry voices suddenly erupted from the table that Silver was playing at.

The drifter had thrown down his cards and started shouting at Silver.

'I reckon you're nothing but a cheat!' he said accusingly. 'No man has as much luck as you, mister.'

'Maybe he's right,' chipped in one of the miners, despite his partner laying a hand on his shoulder to try and placate him.

'How many cards have you up your sleeves? That's what I want to know,' the drifter demanded, thumping the table with his fist and making the money jingle.

The man called Silver merely smiled. He drew out a fresh cheroot from his breast pocket and carefully pierced its side with his toothpick, and then he struck a flame.

'I am going to let that slur pass, for the moment,' he said with a slight drawl. 'Let me give you some advice, friend. There are fifty-two cards in a deck of cards. There are four suits, which means that there are four of every type of card. Four aces, four kings, four . . . '

'I know that!' the drifter snarled.

Silver lit his cheroot, holding it by the toothpick in that unusual, languid way of his. 'Well you also ought to know that extra cards would be pretty easy to spot. And if you ended up with two Ace of Spades, for example, then folks might justifiably get a bit irate.'

'That's what I am,' replied the drifter. 'Irate!'

'Maybe someone could just slide a few aces off the bottom of the deck when they were dealing and add them in later on,' piped in the miner who seemed to have sided with the drifter.

'Perfectly possible,' agreed Silver. 'But I hope that no one is suggesting that I have done any such thing?'

'I sure as hell am!' snapped the drifter, reaching for his gun.

He had drawn quickly, but the gun never reached the horizontal. There was an explosion and a hole appeared in his forehead amid a cloud of smoke. He teetered on his feet and the gun went off, blowing a hole in the table as his body tumbled backwards to crash on to his chair. A thick stream of blood gushed out of the exit wound at the back of his skull, splashing on to the floor.

Silver was still sitting, pointing a smoking Remington Navy Colt at the body.

'My god!' gasped Helen, covering her mouth and doubling up as if she was about to lose the meal that she had just eaten.

'Easy!' Hank said, placing a comforting hand on her shoulder.

He had almost, out of reflex, reached for his own weapon, but forcibly stopped himself. He had to let this scene play out without any interference from him.

People all around had scraped their chairs back and stood up, unsure of what to do.

All except Finlay Macgregor. He came pushing his way through the crowd, a sawn-off shotgun in his two great fists.

'Put that gun away this instant, Silver,' he growled, waving his shotgun menacingly.

Silver very deliberately did as he was bidden. Then he took a puff of his cheroot and with a smile blew out a stream of smoke. 'It was self-defence, Macgregor, everyone saw that. The fool accused me of cheating.' Then slowly he turned to look at the miner who had sided with the dead drifter.

'I don't take kindly to folks that call me a cheat,' he added.

The miner raised his hands. 'I didn't call you nothing, mister. I don't want any trouble.'

'There won't be any trouble, for now,' said Finlay. 'I can't say what a US marshal might say, though. I'll be reporting this death, Silver.'

In response the gambler leaned over the table and pulled the remains of the money towards him. He took only the notes and folded them into a wad, which he pocketed. 'Just be sure to emphasize that it was self-defence,' he replied.

'I think you should leave right now,' Finlay said, his hands firm on the shotgun. 'And I'm not sure I want to see you back here again.'

Silver stood, removed the cheroot from his toothpick and tossed it on the floor at Finlay's feet. 'I am not sure I want to come back.' He pointed at the loose coins on the table and the floor.

'That money should pay for any damage.'

With which, he made his way through the crowd which fell away to give him passage.

'Damn!' said Finlay once he had gone. 'Will some of you help me haul this guy out of here? Damned inconvenient, that's what this is!'

Hank and Helen had made themselves as inconspicuous as possible. When Finlay came back in ten minutes later and set one of his assistants the task of cleaning up the bloody scene of the drifter's violent death, Hank offered to pay him.

'Ah, but you'll need a burro,' Finlay replied.

Hank nodded his head in agreement. 'It went out of my head. I am afraid that horrible shooting rather upset my little brother. We both just want to be on our way.'

'You'll need a burro to carry all your gear. Come on, I'll fix you up.'

Hank had no choice. He didn't want

Finlay Macgregor to think that he and Helen were anything other than what they said they were. And if they just rushed after Silver he would know that only too well.

He just hoped that he would be able to trail the man.

*　　*　　*

Silver had ridden off nonchalantly, but once out of sight of Macgregor's Trading Post he had ridden behind a large outcrop of rocks, dismounted and climbed up on a large boulder. He stayed there for a full five minutes with his rifle trained on the trail to make sure that no one had taken it into their heads to follow him.

In particular he had suspected that the miners he had played poker with might have decided to recoup their money by force. He had no intention of allowing anyone to backshoot him.

By the time that Hank and Helen had started off with their burro laden with mining equipment he had ridden a fair way down the trail. After his initial caution, Silver had made no attempt to cover his tracks.

'What are you planning to do?' Helen asked. 'Overtake him and arrest him?'

He smiled. 'I have no authority to arrest him. Besides, you saw how fast he is with a gun. He would hardly be the sort of man who would just give himself up if I asked him to. No, we just need to follow him and hope that he leads us to the others.'

They saw him several times as they crested various rises. He seemed to be ambling along. When the sun went down over the Pintos, Hank climbed a slight bluff and trained his spyglass on him.

'Looks like he's set on bedding down for the night,' he told Helen when he returned a few minutes later. 'That means that we had better do the same. It could be an early start.'

He saw her look of slight anxiety. 'We'll have some food and then I suggest we take turns to keep a watch, just to make sure he doesn't come back this way, or that no one else is wanting to keep an eye on Silver. I'll take the first watch.'

7

Hank had made coffee and was cooking bacon when Helen awoke. He was aware that she had probably stayed awake all night, even during his watches. He had seen that she only drifted off to sleep about an hour before sun-up.

He guessed that she had not trusted him, which kind of hurt him, although he had no reason to think that she should. After all, he reasoned, he was part of the reason that her fiancé was dead and buried. On top of that he had hardly been honest with her. Even the disguise, such as it was, had been contrived to fool Wilson and the preacher man, Eli Tabner, if and when he saw them, but not for the reason he had given Helen. He was concerned that she would learn his secret from them. He had no doubt that the preacher knew of his supposed part in the hold-up, albeit he had failed to play his part. He was supposed to ensure that Tom and the passengers all surrendered their weapons.

Even thinking about it made him angry, for he was unsure whether they had any intention of letting anyone live in the first place.

'Is it safe to cook breakfast?' she asked him. 'Won't the smell carry to Silver?'

'It doesn't matter if it does,' he replied with a smile. 'We're just two brothers travelling in the Pintos, aiming to go mining. We have every right and reason to be cooking breakfast. If we didn't make a fire that might seem even more suspicious to him.'

'Have you spied on him?'

'I have. He's still there. That's another reason we can enjoy our breakfast. We need him to get a good start on us.'

'Of course, we can hardly overtake him, can we,' she said with the faintest glimmer of a smile. She picked up her canteen and a towel and a small bag. 'I am just going to freshen myself up.'

He nodded and turned the bacon over. 'It'll be ready when you get back. And some good strong Arbuckle's coffee will set us up for whatever the day ahead holds for us.'

He just hoped that Silver would lead them to the others.

★   ★   ★

Hank had never been on this particular trail before. It went right through another series of canyons and eventually emerged from the Pintos and travelled through undulating terrain that became more verdant. Clearly they had entered cattle territory.

'We're going across someone's range now. That makes it likely that Silver is headed for some cattle town.'

'Do you know it?'

Hank shook his head. 'Never been this way before.' He handed her his spyglass. 'He's up ahead all right.

Taking his time.'

'Does he know we're following him?'

'I think he'll definitely know that we're on the same trail, but I don't think he'll consider us a threat.'

'How do you know?'

'Just a feeling. He's got a spyglass, too. From time to time I've spotted the reflection of the sun on it, when he must have looked back. But I reckon if he'd thought we were really tracking him, he'd have hidden and let us pass him. He may even have challenged us.'

'Why wouldn't he think we were a threat? There are two of us.'

'We have a burro, Helen. There is no way we'd have this critter tagging along if we were after him. No, he'll feel safe.'

Hank had no wish to arouse Silver's suspicions. Not when he knew how fast he was with a gun.

* * *

A couple of hours later the trail reached a fork, where a crude sign had been erected. There were two arrows on it, pointing out the two trails. One read simply 'Nowhere.' The other read 'Hope.'

Hank pointed to the fresh tracks and the pile of horse dung a few yards down the trail to Hope.

'Let's hope that we'll get lucky in Hope.'

Helen nodded, but Hank saw the way her jaw muscles had tightened. Perhaps the danger of their mission had become more real for her.

Ten minutes later, when they reached a small creek that marked the boundary of the town of Hope, they both wondered whether the sobriquet had been someone's idea of a joke. It was not the size of the town that made them think this, rather the quality of its buildings. At first sight it seemed to be a sprawling collection of clapboard shops, businesses, adobe-walled dwellings and a substantial number of lean-to structures which looked more suited to chicken rather than human habitation.

The main street was severely S-shaped rather than the straight type that one expected. Hank wondered whether the town founders had designed it deliberately to prevent cattle from stampeding through, or worse, a stampede of high-spirited cowboys after a trail drive.

The thing that it lacked, Hank thought, was a railroad. Hope was a cattle town, all right, but simply one that drives passed close by. It was a 'nearly' town.

As they forded the creek and entered the town, leading the burro behind them, they were met by the inevitable mixed group of urchins and loafers. Most of them kept their distance, pretending to lose interest and strolling off in different directions after they had satisfied their curiosity and found them of little interest.

All except one: a bleary-eyed man in his mid-thirties. He was a thin fellow of medium height with a tangle of red hair, atop which he wore a battered derby hat. He peered at them through thick wire-framed spectacles.

'Howdy, folks, you look like you're going mining.'

Hank tipped his hat. 'We are, sir. I'm Leroy Jones and this is my little brother Billy.'

'Welcome to Hope,' he returned. 'I'm Thaddeus Newman, the editor and proprietor of the *Hope Chronicle*. I'm always interested in news.' He grinned and gestured at the surrounding buildings. 'And as you can probably tell, we don't have too much news in Hope. Can I interest you in a coffee? My office is just up the street.'

Hank looked at Helen and nodded meaningfully. Then he turned back to Thaddeus Newman. 'Why I would appreciate that, Thaddeus. That is right neighbourly of you. But I'm afraid that Billy doesn't like to talk much, so if it's all right with you, I'll step inside for a coffee with you and Billy will just sit out on the porch.'

'Excellent. And maybe I can find some lemonade for Billy. In this heat you need to keep drinking.'

After hitching their horses and burro, Helen pulled out a notepad from her saddle-bag and took a seat on the porch outside the *Hope Chronicle* office. Hank took a lemonade out to her while Thaddeus poured coffee.

'This is a mighty impressive business you have here,' Hank said as he took the seat that the editor offered him.

A printing press, master frame, ink balls, bottles of ink and large piles of paper took up one half of the office. The other half consisted of a desk cluttered with old copies of the *Hope Chronicle* newspaper, writing paper and a pipe rack.

'It serves its purpose,' Thaddeus replied. 'That is, it enables me to keep the good folk of Hope up to date with the news.' He reached for a pipe and filled it from a tobacco jar on the desk. 'The trouble is, there are folks around here who are not overly keen on the news that I choose to print.'

'How so, Thaddeus?'

The editor struck a light and puffed his pipe into life, sending clouds of smoke towards the already yellowed ceiling.

'Not sure how much I should tell you, Leroy,' he said with a wink. 'The thing is that as a newspaperman I like to tell people what I see.

'Everyone has a right to know what's going on in a town. Even strangers like you and Billy.'

'I appreciate your honesty and integrity, Thaddeus.'

'The thing is, I believe that we have a corrupt sheriff and an equally corrupt mayor, who just happens to be the local judge. I can't actually print that, for obvious reasons, but I print stories that may be critical of folks when they deserve to be criticized. It is a fine line that I have to walk.'

Hank looked through the window at Helen and saw that she was busily sketching in her notebook.

'Teaching is my business,' Hank replied. 'But Billy and I are aiming to give ourselves a chance at striking lucky. We're on a sort of mining adventure.'

'Is that so?' Thaddeus asked with a smile. 'The thing is, Leroy, that I consider myself to be a fairly good judge of people. I have to be in my work. And I am pretty good at putting two and two together. You might say I was well taught.' He took off his spectacles and polished the lenses on his sleeve before putting them back on again. 'I took a liking to the two of you when you came into town. But despite the thickness of my spectacles and the deficiency in my vision, I see more than most folk do. For example, I can see that you aren't exactly telling me the truth.'

Hank was sipping coffee and he sat for a moment staring at the editor over the rim of his coffee cup.

'I don't follow you.'

'Well, bear with me and see if I am right. You are not on a mining adventure, are you? If you were you'd be heading into the Pintos, not away from them.'

Hank said nothing but nodded for him to continue.

'And your little brother is fairly petite. More like a sister, I would say. But then again, you have both got blondish hair, but hers is as yellow as corn and yours looks too blond, as if it has been bleached. I'm not sure that you are related at all.' He laid his pipe down in an ashtray. 'And if I'm not mistaken, she's a bit of an artist. I think one of you might be a teacher, but I'd reckon it was' — he coughed delicately — 'Billy. As for you, I think you either are or have been a lawman.'

'It looks as if our disguise didn't work too well, Thaddeus.'

'Oh, I reckon it would fool most folks, but I am a professional busybody. It is my business to see things that don't seem right and work out what is going on. And if I may venture a guess, I'd say that you were looking for someone.'

'You are right, we are.'

'Someone called Silver?'

Hank raised an eyebrow. 'How did you know that?'

'You came into town not ten minutes after him. He will have been to Macgregor's Trading Post, I reckon. I know it is one of his regular haunts, which suggests that you've followed him from there at least.'

'Mind if I call Billy in?'

A few moments later Helen was sitting while Hank explained Thaddeus's deductions.

'Might I ask what you were drawing?' Thaddeus asked.

In answer Helen opened her book and showed him a remarkable likeness of Silver.

'Wow! You have talent, Billy. Or, what should I call you?'

'Just keep calling me Billy,' she replied, 'but my real name is Helen.'

'And it is best if you just call me Leroy,' Hank added. 'You've been good enough to put your cards on the table,

Thaddeus,' he went on confidingly. 'Now let us put ours down as well.'

And between them, they told him about the dry gulching in the Devil's Bones and all about Tom. Hank just hoped that the shrewd editor would not suspect that he was keeping some information back from them.

'I am truly sorry, *Billy*,' Thaddeus said.

'And so we think that Silver was one of the three robbers. I think I'll recognize the one that was masquerading as the preacher Eli Tabner. The third one, we don't know about. We thought that Silver might lead us to them, but of course, we could not afford for me to be recognized by them. Silver probably hadn't seen my face, since he was up on top of the canyon rim, but the preacher and the gunman probably would.'

'And we thought that a woman could attract more attention than a boy,' added Helen.

'Well I reckon you'll find out pretty

soon whether it has worked or not. You saw the way that crowd greeted you. Some of them are paid by the sheriff and the judge to keep them informed about anyone new coming to town. They'll know not only what you look like, but what your horses and burro look like and what they are carrying.'

Helen flashed a worried look at Hank. 'What should we do?'

'I think we just carry on as we planned,' Hank replied. 'Book into a hotel and then have a look around the town.'

'What are your plans?' Thaddeus asked.

'I need to find these men and hopefully take them down, one by one. I'm going to try and take them alive and make sure that they face justice.'

'I'd like to help in any way that I can,' Thaddeus said with a doubtful look. 'The problem is that I am not one for guns. I am pretty sure that if I ever wore one they would use that as an excuse to bump me off.'

'Have they done that before to anyone?'

'Silver has, and the sheriff and the judge let him off. It happened a couple of times and they just arrange for Silver to pick a fight, then . . . ' He let his voice tail off. 'That is why I have to be careful in my stories.'

'What about bringing in the law? Get a US marshal to come and see what's going on?'

Thaddeus shook his head. 'They are the law here. A sheriff and the mayor — who is also the judge. And folks have gotten used to obeying the law. You can imagine that no one ever stands against them come election time. No one even tries to leave town any more. At least not without their say so.'

Helen's eyes widened in horror. 'You mean they hold the town to ransom?'

'Pretty much. And when they are not here, such as when that hold-up took place, they have a bunch of low-life scum who sort of deputize for them.'

Helen shook her head. 'It sounds as if

instead of us trailing Silver, he led us into a trap.'

The editor picked up his pipe and tapped the bowl into the ashtray. 'I am afraid that might be the case. And I don't mean to alarm you, but Silver is coming across the street this minute.'

8

Silver walked straight into the *Hope Chronicle* office and tipped his hat.

'I guess you are the two fellers that have been tagging along behind me, ever since I left Macgregor's Trading Post?' He smiled his suave smile. 'You had only to ask if you wanted to get to know me better.'

Hank forced an obsequious smile. 'Why sir, the truth is that me and my brother Billy did see you at that Trading Post, but we're travelling independently, you might say. We're planning to go mining and we bought some equipment from Mr Macgregor.'

'That little fracas had nothing to do with you following me?'

'No sir. And we're not looking for any trouble, sir. We're just going about our business. And we mind our business, sir.'

'What's wrong with him?' Silver asked, nodding towards Helen. 'Cat got his tongue?'

'Actually, sir, it has. My little brother hasn't spoken since he was six years old, on account of him seeing our father killed in front of his eyes.'

Helen looked petrified and shook her head vigorously.

'My name is Jones, sir. Leroy Jones and I am a teacher by profession. But Billy and me thought we'd try our luck in the hills.'

Silver held up his hands, each of which had two silver rings. 'Well, I can understand the attraction of silver. I kind of like it myself. Folks call me Silver.'

He turned his attention on Thaddeus. 'I expect that you'll be putting a story in your newspaper about these two gents?'

Thaddeus was toying with his unlit pipe. 'I daresay I will, Mr Silver. I daresay I will.'

'Well, that's fine. But just a word of

warning to you. I wouldn't write anything about that fracas I just mentioned. I wouldn't want to read anything like that in your paper.'

He switched his attention back to Hank and Helen. 'So I think you can safely leave that out of whatever story you tell Mr Newman here. We don't want the citizens of Hope to read about untruths.'

And with a tip of his hat, he left.

'Phew! He was just checking you out as well as giving me his customary warning. What happened at Macgregor's, by the way?'

Hank opened his mouth to reply, but Helen beat him.

'He shot a man in the head. And he didn't even bat an eyelid about it.'

* * *

After leaving their horses and burro at the livery Hank and Helen booked into the Hope Hotel, which they learned from the man on the desk was owned by Judge Carlton Stanley. The man was willing to talk and he told them that the judge owned about half the town. Several other businesses were owned by Silver.

Since they were travelling as brothers they booked a single room to avoid making the man suspicious.

'I'll sleep on the floor,' Hank reassured her once they entered the room and set their saddle-bags and Winchesters down on the floor. The mining equipment they left at the livery.

'How can Thaddeus Newman tolerate living here?' Helen asked.

'He seems to have resigned himself to it, I think,' Hank replied. 'In his mind I think he probably believes that he is standing up to them, but he's probably no more than a minor nuisance to them.'

'Do you think that they would stop us leaving town if we decided to go right now?'

'I don't know. We only have what Thaddeus said to go by. One thing is sure, though. We need to work out a plan and we need to put it into action as soon as possible.'

'We saw how fast Silver is with a gun. You were a lawman, so I suppose you must be pretty fast, too. If it came to it, do you think you could beat him?'

Hank rubbed his chin, feeling the stubble. 'I better have a shave or my black stubble may give us away straight away.' He pursed his lips. 'And about my speed — I honestly don't know. If I can take him any other way, I'd rather do that.'

'You mean if 'we' can take him, Leroy!' she said with a smile. 'We are in this together, remember.'

He smiled back. Her use of the word 'we' sounded strangely good. Yet as soon as he thought that, he pushed the idea out of his mind. He could not possibly allow himself to think of Helen in that way, not when he had such a burden of guilt.

'Of course, and I just hope that we will be able to — '

There was a knock on the door and

Hank crossed the room and opened the door. It was the hotel receptionist with a tray with crockery and a coffee pot.

'Coffee and cookies, with the compliments of the Hope Hotel, gentlemen,' he said. 'It is our policy to attend to our guests' every need.'

When he had gone Helen poured them a cup each and offered the cookie plate to Hank.

'I was going to suggest that we get a bite to eat,' he said. 'I was starting to feel hungry. It's been a long time since breakfast.'

They sipped their coffee and ate the cookies.

'You are a gifted artist,' Hank said. 'You caught Silver exactly.'

'I draw or paint whenever I can. I like doing portraits. In fact, I did a miniature one of myself for Tom. He kept it in his watch. I . . . I only wish it hadn't been stolen.'

'Let's hope that we can get it back soon,' he said, taking another sip of coffee.

Then, seeing her face go suddenly very pale, he set his cup down. 'Helen, what's wrong?'

Her eyes rolled upwards and she slumped sideways and fell off the chair on to the floor.

Suddenly, he felt a strange sensation in the back of his throat and the room seemed to start spinning. 'My god! We've been — '

He felt himself falling into a black pool of unconsciousness.

★　★　★

Hank could feel the sun shining on his face and he shut his eyes tight for a moment as he gradually roused. But it felt strange, for normally he was the type of person who awoke instantly and was ready for whatever the day would throw at him. The only other time he had felt as drowsy as this was after he had been shot and —

Helen! The last thing he remembered was Helen falling off her chair. And then he remembered feeling dizzy and he passed out.

There was noise close by. Like people shouting and bawling. It was like a crowd, a mob.

He blinked his eyes open and tried to sit up, but couldn't. He felt as weak as a kitten.

He was aware of something in his hand and managed to raise it in front of his eyes.

To his horror he saw that it was a knife. And it was covered in blood, as was his hand.

Raising his head he saw people staring down at him through the glass panel of a door and through windows upon which he could see the reversed words of the *Hope Chronicle*.

He struggled and managed to raise himself on an elbow and looked to his side. There were newspapers and print debris scattered everywhere as if there had been some sort of a struggle.

With mounting panic he got on to his other elbow and pushed himself up.

Then he saw the body.

Thaddeus Newman was lying sprawled on the floor, a mallet in one hand. His spectacles lay on the floor beside him. But it was his face that filled Hank with horror. His eyes were staring sightlessly up at the ceiling.

His throat had been cut and a huge pool of congealed blood had accumulated all around him.

'Here's Sheriff Slade!' he heard someone cry.

Then there was a bang as the door was kicked open and he found himself staring up at Wilson. He saw the star on his vest and the heavy Peacemakers in both hands.

'You!' he gasped.

But he had no time for anything else as several men rushed in behind the sheriff.

'You murdering dog!' someone cried.

'He's cut Thaddeus Newman's throat,' another yelled.

'Let's not bother with trying the bastard, let's string him up right now!'

There was the explosion of a gun being fired.

'There'll be no lynching in my town,' barked the sheriff, as he stood on Hank's wrist, causing the knife to fall from his hand. 'Now a couple of you, grab an arm each and let's get him over to my office and we'll sling him in a cell. There'll be a trial all right, and then it's likely that he'll hang, but it'll be done legally. I'll see that the judge hears about it myself.'

'You . . . you dog!' Hank began.

But the sheriff raised his gun and struck him across the side of the head with the barrel.

'You'll speak when you are spoken to, you piece of scum.'

Hank slumped down from the blow and felt himself being dragged through the braying crowd towards the sheriff's office.

His main thought was not for himself, but for Helen. What had happened to her?

9

After being disarmed Hank was thrown on to a bunk in a cell by the two men who had been instructed to drag him from the *Hope Chronicle* office. There was the clang of a barred door and the rattle of a key in the lock and then he was left alone.

Think, Hank! Think! He chided himself as he lay there, that he had been so stupid as to allow himself to be drugged and sandbagged in this manner. Now that he thought about it, the coffee had tasted slightly bitter, but the sweetness of the cookies had taken the edge off that. Whatever the drug was it must have been strong to have knocked him out for so long. Or perhaps he had been given more of it while he was unconscious to stop him from waking until the next morning.

Thaddeus Newman had told him that the sheriff and the judge had eliminated people before. And they had used Silver to do so. Well they had certainly killed two birds with one stone this time. They had brutally murdered Thaddeus and they had staged it so that it looked as if Hank had done it.

Now they were talking about a trial. It would be a travesty, of course. Yet surely he would be entitled to a lawyer? And there was no way that he was going to keep quiet about the three of them, murderers that they were.

But what had they done with Helen? That really gnawed away at him. Had they hurt her?

He felt a cold shiver run down his spine. Could they even have killed her?

He started to perspire at the very thought of it. He had failed her completely and utterly.

You fool! You blind fool!

What had he been thinking of in the first place, letting her come with him? A quest like this was no place for a woman. It must have been the head wound that had clouded his thinking. He should simply have stood his ground and refused to take her. Now he was in the worst situation imaginable and he had no idea where she was, or what had happened to her.

He swung his legs off the bed and stomped his boots down hard on the floor.

It was only when he heard the mocking laugh that he realized there was a man standing in the corridor watching him.

It was Wilson, the man who had led him on this path to hell. If he could have reached him he would have throttled the life out of him.

'Well, well, Hank Hawkins, what a surprise it was seeing you here in Hope, especially when we thought we had left you dead at Devil's Knee.'

'You mangy dog!' Hank said, contemptuously. 'You never had any intention of letting anyone on the Concord live.'

Hank looked at the man he had known as Wilson and wondered how he could possibly have been so taken in by him. How could he have thought that he was in any way trustworthy?

The money! That was the reason. He had given him a tidy package of it and Hank had believed that it would be a simple hold-up and no one would get hurt.

Yet as he looked at him he had to admit that there was something about him that made him look dependable. He was the same height as Hank, with broad shoulders and a firm jaw. There was no hint of cruelty in his expression. He looked like a solid, upright town sheriff. That was the identity that he had adopted in Hope. This was the Sheriff Nat Slade that Thaddeus Newman had told him about.

Then a sly smile crossed the sheriff's face and Hank recognized the face of evil. 'You'll never know, will you Hank. Things might have been different if that fool of a messenger hadn't tried to be a hero.'

'Which one of you shot me?'

'Oh that was the judge. Or as you knew him, the preacher, Eli Tabner. He likes acting, does good old Judge Carlton Stanley.'

'So what are you planning now? To have a mock trial and then have me hanged? Well it won't work. You have to let me have a lawyer and I will demand a trial with a proper judge.'

There was another laugh from behind the so-called sheriff and then another man stepped into Hank's view.

It was the preacher, Eli Tabner. At least, it was the same man, but now he was dressed quite differently. He had on a top hat, a high collar and string tie and a frock coat. In one hand he carried a silver-topped cane.

'So this is the man accused of murdering Thaddeus Newman,' he said, peering in at Hank over the top of a pair of pince-nez spectacles. He smiled then let them dangle from a chain around his neck.

'You're the cur that shot me!' Hank exclaimed.

'Have a little respect for Judge Carlton Stanley,' the sheriff said, mockingly.

'Indeed,' said the supposed judge. 'After all, it doesn't make sense to antagonize a man who will have the power of life or death over you, when you are brought in front of me in court this afternoon.'

'This afternoon? You can't be serious. I am entitled to proper legal representation. I need to see a lawyer, a proper lawyer and we'll have this travesty shown for what it is.'

'Oh it will be this afternoon, and it will be a proper trial, I assure you. Everyone knows Judge Stanley to be a fair man. Strict, perhaps, but fair.' He stared at Hank for a moment then sneered. 'But just between the two of us, it was me that shot you, but I am a tad embarrassed at missing the back of your head at such close distance. My aim was impaired by one of Silver's bullets, which went clean through that cowboy. I think it made me jerk and I clearly only grazed you. When you pitched forward with blood spurting the way it did, I rather assumed you had died.'

Wilson grinned. 'I ought to tell you that there isn't another lawyer in town.'

'Then when I defend myself I'm going to tell the whole town the truth about the three of you.'

The judge swung his cane languidly between his finger and thumb. 'Oh, I don't think you will. In fact, if you have any compassion for that charming lady that you have been travelling with, the one that has been masquerading as a boy, then you'll say not a single word. You will admit to your real name and you will admit your crime.'

'What have you done with her?'

The judge reached into a vest pocket and drew out a watch. 'Oh Silver is looking after her for me. He won't harm a hair on her head, as long as you do as you are told. If you murmur anything at all, then she will have her throat cut, before any other special treatment is doled out to her.'

'You dogs!'

The judge opened the watch and stared at it with a smile. 'I rather took to this picture that she painted of herself,' he said, turning it for Hank to see. 'What was it that the messenger — Tom, I think his name was — said about her? 'She's worth dying for.' It was something like that, wasn't it?'

He grinned as he snapped the watch closed. 'What do you think, Hank Hawkins? Is she worth dying for? I must admit that I hope that Silver doesn't have to dispose of her if you do something stupid. I have taken rather a liking to her myself.'

Hank hung his head. 'And if I agree to do what you say, what will happen?'

The judge gave a smile that looked totally benevolent. 'Why simply, she will stay alive. Surely that is all you need to know.'

Hank nodded.

'Excellent, but now the good sheriff and I must get going. He has a case to build, a body to dispose of and I must go and see your young lady and our good friend Silver and prepare for the trial.'

With a swagger of his cane he left.

'And don't think that you can get out of this cell,' said Wilson. 'There's no way those bars can be moved. Besides, one of my deputies will be in that office with a sawn-off shotgun.'

* * *

The trial took place in the ironically named Eternal Hope Church Hall. Judge Stanley presided from behind a table atop the stage with Hank sitting with manacles on his wrists in a chair at the foot of the stage. Twelve citizens had been selected for the jury and seemingly a lot of the town were crammed in and either occupied seats or stood watching and listening as the sheriff, acting as a prosecutor stated the facts of the case.

After Hank had given his real name the judge read out the accusation against him and ended by asking how he pleaded. Hank merely stared back at him and hung his head.

'Cat's got his tongue,' the judge had mocked, peering at him through his pince-nez spectacles. 'A pretty clear sign of guilt, I'd say.'

He questioned the sheriff and made copious notes. Then he allowed the sheriff to question various witnesses.

Throughout it all, Hank remained silent, all too aware that Helen's life depended upon him cooperating with them.

It did not take long. The crowd had all too clearly accepted the evidence, which looked totally damning. There was much murmuring and mumbling as the jury were dispatched into a side room to come to their verdict.

Judge Stanley rapped his gavel for order, when they had filed back in and sat down.

'Chairman of the jury,' he said, addressing the gangly, short-sighted storekeeper who stood up again when the judge started speaking. 'You have all heard the evidence so ably presented by Sheriff Nat Slade. How do you find the defendant?'

'Guilty on all counts, your honour.'

There were cries of jubilation, mingled with shouts for justice.

'Hang him!'

'Cut his throat, like he did to poor Thaddeus.'

'Let the dogs have him first.'

Judge Stanley rapped his gavel several times. 'Order! There will be order in this court. And that is enough of those remarks. I am fully aware that the town has been shocked by this outrage. The sad fact is that the accused's refusal to comment means that we will never know why he murdered our respected newspaper editor, who was such a credit to our community.'

This rhetoric was rewarded by murmurs of approval and agreement.

'But still, there will be no taking of the law into the hands of a mob. The law will follow due process.'

He frowned and rapped his gavel again. 'The accused will stand up.'

Hank did so.

'Hank Hawkins, you have been silent throughout this trial, apart from mentioning your name. That is the act of a despicable coward, sir. But this court has been fair to you and justice will be done. The jury has heard all the evidence and found you guilty. It is now my duty to sentence you.'

He stopped and took a deep breath, as though it pained him to pass sentence.

'I rule that for your crime of cold-blooded murder, you shall be hanged by the neck until you are dead. This sentence will be carried out at nine o'clock tomorrow morning.'

He rapped his gavel. 'This court is now closed. Take him away, Sheriff Slade.'

Hank was manhandled through the

crowd and he accepted without retaliation, several slaps around the head and more than a few gobbets of spit directly in his face, as he was forced through the hostile crowd.

'We look forward to seeing you swing in the morning, you bastard!' someone yelled.

Yet not everyone in the crowd was baying for his blood. There were a few people who had watched with a mounting sense of injustice. They had all been friends of Thaddeus Newman and remained unconvinced that they had seen a fair trial.

10

Helen had no real idea of what was going on.

She had awoken with a dreadful headache, only to find that she was unable to raise her hand to her head. She was lying down and as she attempted to move she perceived that she was on a bed to which she had been lashed down, for she could move neither arms nor legs.

Then she realized that she had a gag in her mouth and a blindfold over her eyes.

Panic threatened to overcome her, but as a cool-headed young woman she knew that would serve no purpose. She therefore forced herself to remain as calm as possible.

Somewhere close by she heard a floorboard creak and she realized that she was not alone.

Where was Hank? Had he been drugged like her?

Then she remembered the coffee and the cookies.

Could she still be in the hotel? It was more than possible, she realized, since the bed did not feel too uncomfortable.

But what was whoever had drugged them intending to do with her.

She felt something cold pressed against her temple and the noise of something ratcheting.

'I am going to take the gag from your mouth,' came a man's voice. 'Make a single noise and I will pull the trigger and you will never hear anything again in your life. Nod your head if you understand.'

Helen did as she was bid and felt the gag being removed.

'Now I'm going to pour some drink in your mouth. Swallow it, or I'll fire.'

She felt a bottle being placed on her lips, then liquid was poured into her mouth. It tasted awful and she almost gagged.

'Swallow!'

She did and before she could even think of asking a question the gag was replaced and pulled tight.

'That's the way. You'll sleep some more, and when the time is right, someone is coming to have a little chat with you.'

The voice seemed to trail off and she felt herself falling fast asleep.

*   *   *

Although Hank had just about resigned himself to his fate, for he knew that he was to die ignominiously by the rope, his mind had not stopped racing.

Helen! Where was Silver holding her? He had played his part and had not said a word in the court, for fear that it would mean Helen's life, yet he felt torn apart in the knowledge that even if they let her live, it would be at a horrific cost. And even then he had little doubt that when they had tired of her, she too would be murdered.

Those dry gulchers had much to answer for and it grieved him that he was impotent to do a thing about it. Yet he could not afford to give up hope that something would present itself.

Cal Ryker, the deputy who had been detailed to look after him was a drinker. He smelled of it and from time to time Hank could hear a bottle being uncorked and slurped.

'If I were you, I'd start making peace with your maker,' he advised, when he had pushed a mug of lukewarm coffee under the bars of the cell. 'After what you did, you are as sure as anything going to be on your way to hell at nine o'clock tomorrow morning.'

Hank nodded. 'I guess you may be right. Could you get me a bible?'

The deputy looked back with bleary, bloodshot eyes. 'A bible? Me? Hey, mister, do I look like the sort of man who goes to church?'

'I just assumed you were, when you gave me that advice,' Hank replied, sipping his tepid coffee. 'I always find that reading a bit of the bible helps when I need to feel closer to my maker.'

'You don't say? Well then, once the sheriff gets back I'll see what I can do. I'll have to check that it's all right with him first.'

'Of course you have to.'

'Personally, I don't see what harm it could do. The thing is, who knows what really happens when you die?'

'You sound like a doubting man, deputy.'

'Guess I am. That's why I like to drink. The questions don't hurt as much when you drink. I mean, I don't keep asking the same question over and over.'

'You mean is there a heaven and is there a hell? And do you always just go to one or the other when you die?'

'You got it!'

'But you'll find out when you die, deputy,' Hank replied, adopting a sympathetic tone. 'That is, you'll find out if there really is something. If there isn't, then . . . '

'Then I won't know nothing.' The deputy looked miserable. 'It don't seem fair, somehow, if that is the case. See, that's my problem about church and the bible. How do I know that there is anything in it? How do I know that the preachers ain't just lying?'

'Maybe you should take my place tomorrow,' Hank said with a wry grin.

The deputy looked blankly at him for a moment, then slapped his knee and laughed heartily. 'Don't think I'm so drunk that you'll get me into trading places. I ain't drunk.'

'It was worth a try, deputy. You can't hold that against me, can you? But if you could get me a bible, I'd appreciate it.'

* * *

Helen felt as though she had been asleep for days when she awoke again. But this time she woke and was instantly afraid. Not afraid so that she started moving around in desperation, for she remembered immediately that she was tied, gaged and blindfolded.

She woke and didn't move a muscle, for she had no wish to have more of that awful drug, whatever it was, forced down her.

She just lay there and listened.

There was someone in the room.

Whoever it was, was smoking a cigar and sounded as if they were playing cards.

It was a man playing solitaire.

It just had to be the man called Silver, she deduced. He had been allocated to watch her, which meant that the other two, the sheriff and the judge were taking care of Hank.

Maybe they had already done so?

At the thought of that she felt her heart start to beat faster and she realized that it mattered to her if they had harmed him.

But as the methodical snap of card on card continued, she reasoned that was not likely to be the case. Surely Silver would only be watching her and

146

keeping her drugged until they had dealt with him. And that implied to her that they planned to do something soon. Surely they wouldn't just keep her drugged indefinitely?

No, they wanted her drugged until a certain time.

And since they were still watching her, that must mean that Hank was still alive.

She felt herself relax at the thought.

So for the moment, there was nothing that she could do.

Just lie there and pretend to be asleep.

★　★　★

The judge and the sheriff both came to see Hank after an hour or so. They let Deputy Ryker head off on his quest to get Hank a bible. Then once they were alone, they stood outside his cell.

'You did well, Hank,' the sheriff said, gloatingly. 'Keeping silent was your best hope for the woman.'

147

Judge Stanley stood swinging his cane between finger and thumb, as he had done before. 'Yes, it was a good performance.'

Hank looked at them both in disgust. 'You are a pair of low life scum. You are the actors, pretending to be upholders of the law, when you are just common thieves and murderers.'

The judge laughed. 'Oh come, Hank, you have to admit that there is nothing common about us. We have built the perfect covers for our rather exceptional talents.'

'I'd rather you didn't call me Hank. Only my friends call me that and arranging to have a man hanged is hardly what I'd call friendly.'

Sheriff Slade fixed Hank with a stern look. 'You ought to have more respect for Judge Stanley, Hawkins. Maybe I'll teach you a lesson in manners before we string you up.'

'Why should I listen to you? What more can you do to me than hang me?'

The judge interjected with a smile

that looked positively reptilian. 'We can arrange for it to be a clean hanging that breaks your neck real quick — or you can just dangle! A man can take a long time to die by strangulation. Believe me, it is not pretty.'

'I am guessing you have done this before. Sent men who crossed you to their deaths on trumped up charges?'

'The town doesn't know that,' he returned. 'I told you, we are exceptional men. Both of us are well respected in our town.'

'And what about your trained killer, Silver? Is he respected?'

Judge Stanley gave a knowing smile. 'Let's just say that folks keep a respectable distance from him.'

'Do you really think that you can control a man like him forever?'

'We are friends as well as business colleagues.'

'You are vicious scum,' Hank returned vehemently.

Sheriff Slade put a hand on the butt of his gun. 'Do you want me to soften him up a little?'

'Ah, so we have the truth there,' said Hank with a hint of glee. 'So the so-called judge is really the boss and the sheriff is just the hired muscle.'

'I'm warning you!' Slade growled.

The office door opened and there was the sound of people entering.

'Sheriff Slade, I've got good news,' Deputy Ryker called out. 'Look what I've got.'

And a moment later he appeared in the corridor leading to the cell.

'I did better than just get a bible for the condemned man. I got him a preacher, too.'

The sheriff flashed a look of alarm at the judge, but the judge patted the sheriff's shoulder and gave him a reassuring nod of the head.

'Excellent, deputy. Well done,' he said. 'Well, I had better go, I have things to do, cases to prepare for and a stack of paperwork.'

He turned to Hank. 'You would do well to remember what I just told you,

Hank Hawkins. You have committed a dreadful crime and you are going to pay with your life. As I am sure the Reverend Hooper will tell you, the bible says 'a life for a life!' You understand me, I take it.'

Hank looked up at him and nodded. 'I understand clearly, Judge Stanley. It is as if you had written that in letters of silver.'

The ghost of a smile played across the judge's lips at Hank's reference to Silver. He tapped his cane on the floor. 'Repent of your sins with the Reverend Hooper now.'

'Do you want me to stay with the preacher, sheriff?' Deputy Ryker asked, his eyes even more bleary.

'No, that won't be necessary,' Slade returned. 'You just stay in the office and let the man say his peace with the Lord. I'm heading off for some food. Get the preacher a chair so he can sit comfortable and talk through the bars of the cell.'

A few moments later Hank rested

back on his bunk while he listened to the Reverend Hooper say a prayer for him.

The Reverend Tobias Hooper was a middle-aged man with a pronounced stoop, thinning hair and a wispy beard. He had a gentle disposition and an anxious manner about him.

'Would you like to make a confession, Mr Hawkins?' he asked.

Hank shook his head. 'I am not going to confess to something that I didn't do. I never killed Thaddeus Newman. I just want to maybe read a bit of the bible and make my peace with the Lord before I get hanged.'

The preacher leaned forward in his chair and whispered: 'I know you didn't do it and I would like to help you if I can.'

Hank's eyes widened and he too leaned forward. 'You help me just by believing in me. But how come you do?'

'One of my flock, Chester Jenkins, a man who has known better times, was sleeping off a surfeit of alcohol behind a horse trough. He . . . he saw the man called Silver carry a body into the Hope Chronicle offices in the middle of the night. We think it may have been you. We fear that poor Thaddeus Newman had already been murdered.'

He coughed and opened his bible and read loudly a couple of passages from his bible, for the benefit of Deputy Hooper.

'Why didn't anyone say anything at the trial?'

'Mr Hawkins, those three men and their ruffians have this town in their power. It would have been death for anyone to say anything. A number of us, all Thaddeus's friends have been wondering how we can free ourselves for some time, but none of us are any use with guns.'

'Could you get me a gun?'

The preacher shook his head. 'I am afraid not. I could not carry a lethal weapon like a gun or a knife.' He pulled up a leg of his pants up and reached down into his boot. 'But perhaps this could help. It is yours, anyway.'

For the first time in many, many hours, Hank saw that there might still be a glimmer of hope in the town of Hope.

11

Helen lay still, listening to the slap of cards on the table. She found the smell of cigar smoke quite unpleasant and wished that Silver would open a window or leave the room to allow the air to become less acrid.

Not knowing what time of day it was added to her sense of alarm. She sensed that she had been drugged for many hours, but really had no way of knowing, for the only things she recalled were the moment that she fell unconscious after the coffee and cookies, and some hours ago when she was made to drink more of the drug.

Suddenly there was the rattle of a key in a lock and a door opened.

'How has she been?' came a voice she did not recognize. 'Has she come round at all?'

'Not since that last dose, but I reckon

it would make sense to give her more soon.'

'Actually, I want to talk to her first, then we'll give her more before we move her.'

'We're moving her after dark, right?'

'Yes. Just as you moved him.'

Silver laughed. 'So in the morning he's going to be out of our hair.'

Helen gritted her teeth. So Hank was still alive, but they had taken him somewhere when it was dark. That meant that she must have been unconscious for almost a whole day. But what did they mean that he would be out of their hair? Were they planning to kill him soon?

And why did this new man want to talk to her?

'I think I'll see if I can talk to her now. I'll wake her up while you go and see how our esteemed sheriff is getting on. I think he is a little over-keen on giving our friend a little pistol-whipping.'

'Don't do anything else with her,' Silver said. 'She's a real looker and we have a deal, remember.'

The other man gave an evil laugh. 'Oh don't worry, Silver. We are all friends and partners. Share and share alike. All I am going to do is talk to her.'

Silver grunted and Helen heard boots crossing the room. The door opened and he went out. She heard footsteps diminishing, as if he was going downstairs.

'And now, let's see if you are awake,' came the voice.

And she felt a hand on her shoulder, gently shaking her. She was not sure whether to feign continued unconsciousness or not. Then she reasoned that to do so merely prolonged her state of ignorance about things. She needed to know what they were planning and where they were going to take her. She needed to know something if she was to have any hope of escaping from this plight.

'Time to wake up, my pretty little thing,' the man said in a lascivious tone that made her cringe.

She had little doubt already about what Silver and he had meant when they talked about sharing. They planned to share her.

Then she felt the blindfold being removed from her eyes. She tried looking through her eyelashes and saw a well-dressed man in a frock coat and a top hat. In one hand he was holding a silver-topped cane.

He laughed. 'So you are awake,' he said with a grin. 'I would suggest that you open your eyes properly, that way you will see me better.'

Helen tried to say something, but all that came out was a sort of moaning, because of the gag.

'I am afraid that I cannot remove this gag,' he said. 'I can't have you screaming or trying to shout anyone for help, can I? You see, I think it is time that you and I had a little talk — in private.'

He laid his cane and top hat down on a desk and brought a chair over beside the bed.

'There, that is more comfortable, for you, isn't it? That way you don't have to strain your eyes looking up at me. And it is a chance for the two of us to get to know each other better. And believe me, my dear, we are going to get to know each other very well.'

Her eyes must have alerted him to the shock, revulsion and fear that was mounting inside her.

It did not put him off. He purred like a cat and leant forward to stroke her cheek.

'Such soft skin. You really are a beauty, you know, despite the man's clothes that you were wearing to disguise yourself.'

He reached into a pocket of his vest and took out a watch. He smiled as he held it up for her to see.

'You recognize this, I think. Yes, I can see that you do.'

He opened it and turned it so that she could see her picture.

'Your young man left this for me,' he said. 'He wanted me to have it, actually.

Just as he said that he wanted me to have you.'

Helen looked aghast and struggled against her bonds.

'But don't worry about what Silver said. I think you were listening, weren't you? We are going to move you someplace later tonight. Somewhere much more elegant than this, where you will be able to have fewer restrictions. But there will be no sharing, my dear. You will be mine. Only mine. Like your young man wanted.'

Helen moaned and shook her head.

'Oh yes, you will.' He laughed and reached out with his free hand to caress her neck, letting his hand stray further down her chest. 'Do you know what he said? He said that you were worth dying for.'

He laughed again, a sinister noise that sent a shiver up her spine.

'That was just before he died!'

* ★ ★

Hank had talked with and listened to the preacher, Tobias Hooper. In a way he felt sorry for the townsfolk. The majority did not actually realize that they were really captives of the trio of thieves and their unwitting henchmen. The small handful who did had no means of fighting back. There was no telegraph station and no way that anyone could leave without telling the sheriff. They had apparently imposed that ruling, with the explanation that the sheriff needed to know where anyone was going in case he had to come and get them out of trouble. Those who had gone off on their own had simply never been heard of again.

It was also clear that if Hank could somehow get free he would not be able to get help from the group, who were all too scared of the consequences and of any reprisals that would ensue.

Deputy Ryker had been sent home when the sheriff returned. It was after dusk and the sheriff lit a couple of oil lamps and with one he came through to bait Hank again.

He sat in the chair that the preacher had vacated, drinking coffee laced with whiskey from a bottle of rye that he placed on the floor alongside the cell keys. Hank stared at the keys and then his attention was caught by the whiskey bottle's distinctive label for a moment.

'I guess you'd like a slug of whiskey?'

Hank shook his head. 'I need to keep a clear head for tomorrow morning.' He was well aware that the keys and the bottle had been placed deliberately just out of his reach if he had the opportunity to stretch an arm through the bars to get them.

Slade laughed. 'You know, you are no better than us,' he said, as he savoured his coffee. 'You took that money I gave you and you were prepared to have them all robbed. What did you say it was for, so that you could buy a spread or a farm somewhere?'

He laughed and slurped some coffee.

'Some ambition you had. To be a dirt farmer.'

'I made a mistake,' Hank conceded. 'But I am nothing like any of you. I am no murderer.'

'No? But that isn't quite true, is it? You've done your share of killing. You were a lawman, weren't you? And you had been responsible for the death of your deputy and a young kid who called you out.'

Hank's head snapped up. 'How did you know any of that?'

'We make it our business to know everything before we pull off a job. We knew all about your past, which is why I singled you out and recruited you. You were easy meat.'

Hank shook his head. 'I wasn't responsible for my deputy's death and that young kid wouldn't submit to arrest. I was doing my duty. I didn't like it so I quit the law. But that doesn't mean that I am like any of you. You murdered all those men in cold blood. There is blood on the hands of all three of you.'

There was a knock on the office door and the noise of boots crossing the office and coming down the hall.

Silver grinned as he appeared. He struck a Lucifer and lit a cigar. 'The judge is looking after our little flower and he sent me to make sure that you didn't have any idea of helping Hank on his way to hell before his appointed time with the hangman.'

Slade guffawed. 'Why, all I am doing is trying to cheer his spirits up.'

'How is she?' Hank asked.

Silver blew out a cloud of blue smoke. 'She's well cared for and will remain so as long as you keep your mouth shut when you put your head through that noose tomorrow morning.'

'Let her go,' Hank pleaded. 'She has no part in all of this.'

Silver and Slade looked at each other and laughed.

'Hell, you should just be grateful that she's going to live,' said Slade.

Silver reached down for the whiskey

bottle, uncorked it and took a swig before returning it to the floor.

'What have you told her?' Hank asked.

'About you? Nothing,' Silver replied. 'She's been sleeping a lot of the time. Well, all of the time, to tell you the truth. The judge is actually going to talk to her now.'

'Ah yes, your boss told you to come over here with the other paid help.'

'He isn't the boss, we are all partners,' Sheriff Slade snapped, tetchily.

'What is he talking to her about, then?' Hank probed.

'Possibly he's telling her about you,' Silver said with a smile. He was all too aware that Hank was trying to cause dissent among them. 'I guess she doesn't know that you were in on the robbery.'

'I wasn't in on what you planned to do right from the start.'

'She'll be real disappointed in you when she finds out,' Slade jibed. 'And she's going to know that you were responsible for her man's death.'

Hank felt a wave of guilt well up within him, but it was contained by the anger and loathing that he felt for the two men on the other side of the cell door. 'Maybe she will. I surely don't feel proud of what I did. Anyways, that's what I told the preacher.'

Silver's eyes widened. 'You told who?' Then before he could answer he turned angrily to Slade.

'Did you let him confess to the goddamned preacher?'

'We let him see the preacher. That is, the judge and I let him, because we knew he wouldn't risk telling him anything about us.'

'Damn!' said Silver, punching one fist into the open palm of his other hand. 'Well, we can't take the risk. The preacher will have to have an accident. Tonight!'

Hank cursed himself for mentioning the Reverend Hooper. 'I didn't tell him anything.'

'We don't take chances,' returned Silver. 'I'll wait a few hours then pay him a visit.'

'He's no threat to you,' Hank persisted. 'He doesn't know anything. I wouldn't jeopardize Helen's safety. Please, just let him be. All we did was say a few prayers and he read to me from the bible.'

Silver took a puff on his cigar and let smoke escape slowly from his lips. 'I wouldn't have figured you as a religious man.'

'I have my moments. And the night before my hanging is one of those.'

Slade sipped his coffee. 'I suppose we ought to let the condemned man choose what breakfast he wants.' Then he guffawed and added: 'As long as it is cold beans and cold coffee.'

Hank clicked his tongue. 'I'm not too bothered about breakfast, but I do have a request.' His eye fell on the bottle of whiskey.

Slade saw the look and shook his head. 'This is good whiskey and I'm not wasting it. Besides, we also want you to have a clear head.'

'I didn't mean that,' Hank replied. 'That cigar sure smells good. What's the harm in giving a condemned man a last cigar?'

Silver considered the question for a moment. 'I don't see a problem with that.' He reached inside his vest and drew out a cigar. He tossed it through the bars and Hank deftly caught it. He raised it to his nose, sniffed all the way along its length, and then carefully bit the end off it.

'A light?'

Silver blew on his own cigar to get the tip glowing, then held it towards Hank, just outside the bars of the door so that Hank had to get his face against the bars and light it from the end.

Soon it was going well and Hank stood with it in his mouth, facing Silver through the cell door. 'That's good,' he said. 'Mind if I sit again?'

Silver gestured assent and Hank took

the cigar from his mouth and turned as if about to sit.

There was a sudden fizzing noise and Hank turned round again, a cigar in one hand and stick of dynamite with its fizzing fuse in the other. He tossed the cigar into Sheriff Slade's lap and instantly shot a hand through the bars to draw Silver's gun from his holster.

'Hold it! Both of you!' Hank cried. 'One move and I'll shoot. Take your gun out Wilson, or Slade, whatever you call yourself. Put it on the floor and kick it over here. Quickly, or by God, I am going to take the two of you with me to kingdom come.'

'Easy, Hawkins,' Slade gasped as he lay down his coffee cup and slowly straightened up. 'Don't do anything stupid.'

Silver took the cigar from his mouth and held his hands at shoulder height. 'What do you aim to do, Hawkins?'

'The gun, now!'

The sheriff gingerly removed the gun and placed it on the floor and then he kicked it towards the cell.

'Now open this door!'

Again the sheriff bent to the ground and reached out for the bunch of keys. But at the last moment, instead of picking them up he grabbed the whiskey bottle and brought his arm up, tossed it through the bars. It missed Hank but arched past him and smashed against the wall. With Hank distracted, he jack-knifed down, grabbed the gun and brought it back up towards Hank, ratcheting back the hammer as he did so.

But he was too slow. Hank fired twice in rapid succession, both shots hitting him in the chest. He was thrown back against the wall, blood gushing from two chest wounds. Then he started to slide down it, leaving a trail of blood against the wall.

Silver had also started to move. He snapped his left hand down, throwing the derringer that he always kept concealed in his sleeve into his waiting hand. He pulled back the hammer and trained it on Hank.

But Hank had seen the movement in the corner of his eye and swivelled, still with the fizzing dynamite stick in one hand, the fuse getting perilously close to ignite the dynamite. He shot at the same moment that Silver did and felt a stab of pain shoot across his left upper arm.

For a moment his concern was not to drop the dynamite and he looked down at it.

Silver cried out in pain and his derringer fell from his hand. As Hank looked up he saw the gambler dash for the corridor.

'Damn!' Hank exclaimed. He knew that he couldn't reach the keys, which lay against the wall beside the dead body of the sheriff. He pointed the gun at the lock and fired twice at it.

It gave way and with a kick the door swung open.

He thought of giving pursuit to Silver, yet he knew that the gambler may well have picked up a gun from somewhere in the office and, although he had heard the door being thrown open, he knew that if he gave chase he could well simply run into a hail of lead outside.

He only had one bullet left so desperate measures were needed. He grabbed the dead sheriff's gun, tossed the dynamite into the cell and took cover further along the corridor.

In a few seconds everything would be decided.

12

Helen felt her skin cringe at the man's touch.

He had lit an oil lamp and by its light he had seemed even more sinister. Even more repulsive.

'You will grow to like me,' he said as he continued to caress her neck.

Then he leaned towards her, his lips slightly puckered as if he intended to kiss her.

She tried to shy away from him, but it was not possible.

There was a creaking noise as if someone had stepped on a loose floorboard. Then behind him she saw a shadow, then a figure loomed behind him. She recognized him as Seth Boyd, the old man from the livery, and he had something in his hand. It looked like a pair of metal tongs. There was a whistle as it was swung through the air, followed instantly by a dull thud and the man who had been molesting her slumped forward across her.

'Darn!' the man said, immediately grabbing the body and rolling it on the floor. 'I'll get you out, miss,' he said, removing first her gag, before producing a knife and starting to cut through her ropes.

Helen gulped in air and muttered profuse thanks.

'Don't worry none about thanking me, Miss. The thing we've got to do is get you out of here before the judge comes round again. There will be hell to pay, but we couldn't stand by and let them get away with whatever they had in mind doing to you. It's bad enough that they've got half the town hoodwinked, but killing Thaddeus Newman and framing your friend for it is too much. I'm not sure we can do anything to stop the hanging in the morning, but at least we can get you on your way out of town.'

Helen sat up as he released the last of

the ropes. She automatically started rubbing her wrists to try to ease the discomfort from the ropes that had bound her so tightly.

'Hanging?' she gasped. 'Hank? Are they going to hang Hank? Did . . . did you say that Thaddeus Newman was murdered?'

'I did, but come on; we've got to get you out of here. I've got your two horses saddled and ready. Forget the burro. I'll go with you aways, to show you the way back to the Pintos. There's a full moon out so you'll have to go by that.'

The Reverend Hooper was waiting at the livery. 'Good, you managed to free her, Seth. What about the judge?'

'He'll be waking up soon, I guess. I didn't have time, nor the guts to tie him up.'

'Then we must get the young lady away as soon as possible,' the preacher said.

'I can't go without Hank!' Helen exclaimed.

There was the sound of gunfire.

Several shots rang out, then a few moments later there was a deafening explosion.

'I am afraid that you will really have to go now, Miss,' he said. 'I fear that your friend has just died.'

* * *

Silver had taken up a position in a dark alley opposite the sheriff's office. He had bound a handkerchief around his left hand where Hank's shot had gouged a chunk of flesh from the edge of his palm. He had pulled a Volcanic carbine from the rack and had loaded it while he waited for Hank to dash out in pursuit. He had been waiting with it trained on the door.

The explosion was followed by flames and smoke appearing in the sheriff's office. He shielded his head with his arms, then he waited a few moments before firing at random into the doorway.

'Help!' he called. 'The prisoner has

escaped and he's shot the sheriff.'

People had started to spill out of the saloons and homes into the street.

'What caused that explosion?' Deputy Hooper called, running towards the office. 'How do you know he's not dead in there?'

'Take a look yourself,' replied Silver angrily. 'If you can get in there with that fire going on.'

The deputy and several other men disappeared round the back of the office building.

'I reckon he's escaped all right,' Deputy Hooper announced to the growing crowd when he returned a few moments later. 'He got dynamite from someplace and he blew a hole in the back of the jail. The sheriff has bought it, I reckon.'

He took off his hat and spat. 'Guess we'd best search for the murdering dog and probably get a posse up.'

There was the sound of horses breaking into a gallop and the crowd ran down and round the bend in time to see two riders heading along Main Street in the opposite direction.

Silver had already broken into a run. He headed back to the Hope Hotel. He charged in and bounded up the stairs two at a time.

Judge Carlton Stanley staggered out of the room in which they had kept Helen a prisoner.

'The bitch has escaped!' he growled. 'Some sonofabitch knocked me out and let her get away. What the hell was that explosion and that gunfire?'

'Some other sonofabitch gave Hawkins a stick of dynamite. Wilson is dead, shot by Hawkins and he escaped by blowing a hole in the jailhouse wall.'

'Come on, let's get them. They're both going to suffer.'

'That drunken Deputy Hooper is going to organize a posse. Hawkins and the girl just rode out of town.'

'You fool! Posse be damned! We can't do what we need to do with other folk around. You and me have to handle this ourselves. Go and tell that deputy fool to just get the fire under control and deal with the sheriff's body. Then meet me at the livery.' He put a hand to an enlarging lump on the back of his head. 'Then once we've dealt with them we'll find out who helped them and deal with them too!'

★ ★ ★

Hank had put his hands over his ears as he had hidden behind the corridor wall. He knew that there was a good chance the explosion could smash the wall and without protection he could shatter his eardrums.

When the dynamite exploded and the fire started he staggered as fast as he could through the cell and out of the hole in the back wall of the jail, into the blissful open air.

His ears were ringing, but he didn't think that they were damaged. He held a gun in each hand and looked right and left in case Silver had run round from the front.

There was a man standing signalling to him at the entrance to an alley. He had his hands raised and he was weaponless.

'I'm Chester Jenkins. The preacher said he'd told you about me,' he said softly, once Hank had joined him and they had run up the alley into a back street.

'He told me to watch the jail in case there was an explosion. He said you might try to blow yourself up.'

'I blew myself out,' Hank corrected. 'Do you know where . . . ?'

'Where they've got your lady friend? Sure I do. And if things went the way that Seth Boyd planned, she should be at the livery about now. You've got to get her out of Hope, mister.'

'Show me the quickest way.'

Keeping to the back alleys they made it to the S-shaped Main Street and crossed unseen to the livery. There, with minimum explanation, he leapt into the saddle of the horse that Seth had been planning to ride to show Helen the way.

'Do you know which way to go?' Seth asked.

'Mister, I drive a stagecoach for a living. When I see a road once, I know it forever. In this moonlight I'll have no trouble.'

He looked down at the stooped frame of the preacher, Tobias Hooper. 'Thank you, preacher,' he said with a grateful nod. 'That present you gave me came in mighty handy.'

'I wasn't sure how you would use it, but I am pleased to see that you will not suffer the fate they had planned for you. Now go, Mr Hawkins, before they bring a fearful retribution down on our heads.'

'Don't you worry about that,' Hank said, cursorily checking his saddle-bag to ensure that he had all he needed. 'I can almost guarantee that they'll be coming after us.'

'Then let's ride,' said Helen. Let's ride like the wind.'

★ ★ ★

They rode as fast as the night conditions would allow them. Yet they knew that they could not afford to stop to make camp. If they were being followed, which was undoubtedly the case, then their pursuers would be doing their best to catch up with them as soon as possible.

As they rode they told each other of their respective ordeals. Hank tied a bandanna round the flesh wound on his arm.

'That man who called himself a judge had Tom's watch, Hank,' she said in finishing. 'And he said that Tom said I was worth dying for. How could he have known that?'

'He was the one pretending to be a preacher,' Hank explained. 'He tried to shoot me in the back of the head, but he was jolted at the moment he fired. He only grazed the side of my head.'

'Thank goodness for that,' she said with a shiver.

Hank thanked her and they rode in comparative silence for some hours until the sun started to peep over the tops of the Pintos.

'Can you smell that?' Hank said after they had covered another mile.

'Smoke?'

'Breakfast, maybe,' he replied. 'We'll be at Macgregor's soon enough.'

And indeed, fifteen minutes later Macgregor's Trading Post loomed ahead.

'Do you think we can afford to stop, Hank? Couldn't that give them time to catch us up?'

'I think we are safe enough, Helen. I reckon that we made much better time than them. I have been listening hard and they are nowhere near us. Besides, I need to talk to Macgregor about something.'

The trading post had no customers that early. The tantalizing aroma of frying steak and bacon greeted them as soon as they opened the door.

Macgregor himself was behind his bar, in the process of watering down several bottles of whiskey. He was wearing his derby hat at the same slight angle as before.

'Ah, increasing your profits, I see, Mr Macgregor,' said Hank, accusingly.

Totally unembarrassed by Hank's question Macgregor stared at them with narrowed eyes.

'Why if it isn't my two friends, Leroy and Billy. Although Billy seems to be a woman now.' He shrugged as if it was of no matter. 'The truth is that I was not expecting to see you back here so soon. I thought that the two of you were going to make your fortune.'

'Well that is what we said, I admit,' agreed Hank. 'But you knew otherwise, didn't you, Macgregor?'

This time the Scotsman's expression hardened and the semblance of a smile vanished from his lips. 'What are you getting at?'

'I am saying that you knew damned well that we weren't who we claimed to be.'

Hank was deliberately goading the trading post owner, which he knew could be risky. After all, it had been there that he had clandestinely met with Wilson and agreed to be part of the hold-up plan. He wasn't sure whether the big man recognized him from then, but it was a risk that he felt he had to take.

'That is no big deal,' Macgregor said. 'I have a lot of folk pass through here who don't want their real names to be known. But again, I could see that you were spying on one of my best customers.'

That was what Hank wanted to hear.

'You mean Silver! And that was why you sent someone after us, wasn't it? You gave orders to warn Silver that we had been following him once we got to Hope.'

'I'm not sure that I like your tone, my lad. But as I just said, he is one of my best customers.'

'As are Sheriff Slade and Judge Stanley?'

Helen had been silent throughout the conversation and she was starting to get concerned. She could see that Hank was deliberately provoking Macgregor, and she was not sure with what purpose.

'They are good, respectable people,' Macgregor said.

'I guess you don't water down the sheriff's whiskey like you are doing with those bottles. I saw a bottle of your whiskey in his office.'

'So? I am a businessman. I sell things.'

Hank's hands had strayed downwards and were hovering not far from the butts of the guns in his waistband.

'So they are just customers, too, are they Macgregor? That's hogwash and you know it. You are in cahoots with them and the lot of you are crooks. You trade supplies for stolen goods that they bring you.'

Macgregor smiled then wiped the bar top with a cloth. As he did so Hank noticed the ring that he was wearing on his right hand. He had not been wearing it the last time they had been there, but he recognized it nonetheless.

'Interesting ring that you have there, Macgregor. It looks identical to the one that one of my passengers was wearing when your partners held us up at the Devil's Knee.'

Macgregor's hand dropped below the surface of the bar and reappeared instantly with a sawn-off shotgun.

'Damn your eyes!' he cried as he raised it towards them.

But Hank drew and fired twice in rapid succession.

The first bullet ploughed into the big man's chest, throwing him backwards against the rows of bottles, with blood gushing from a wound. The second went through his forehead, causing his derby hat to go flying.

'Hank!' Helen gasped. 'Was he really going to shoot us?'

'No doubt at all. He was an important part of their operation and I'm sure that there was blood on his hands.'

Two people came rushing out of the

kitchen. They were the couple who assisted Macgregor and who had served them last time. They looked horrified when they saw the body of their boss sprawled against the back counter, covered in blood, and Hank standing with a gun in his hands. They put up their hands immediately.

'Me and my . . . my wife only work for him,' the young man volunteered. Hank remembered his tousled hair and his crop of spots.

'Please, don't shoot,' his wife pleaded. 'We don't want any trouble.'

'Were you the one who followed us and told Silver about us?'

The man looked terrified. He swallowed hard and nodded. 'But that's all I did, sir. I . . . I came straight back.'

Hank pointed at the door. 'Go! Both of you go now. Is there anyone else in the building?'

'Only us,' the wife replied.

'Then go and get two horses and hightail it out of here. Only don't go to either Hope or to Hastings Fork.'

Hank shoved the gun back in his waistband. 'Time for us to go too. I guess you aren't hungry anymore, so just get some jerky from over there and a couple of tins of beans and some coffee.'

She did as he said while he went over to Macgregor's body.

'I am taking this ring as evidence,' he told her as he pulled it from the dead man's hand. 'Now you go out as well and take our horses over to the corral and wait.'

'What are you going to . . . ' she began. Then she saw him take out a stick of dynamite from under his vest.

'He sold us two sticks, remember? I used the one that the Reverend Hooper gave me to get out of the jail and this one the liveryman kindly left in my saddle-bag. 'Go, I'll give it a couple of minutes then I'll come running.'

True to his word, exactly two minutes later Hank came out of the trading post and sprinted to the corral.

The trading post blew apart and

thick smoke started belching out of the burning building.

The young couple had saddled a pair of horses and were about to leave.

'He was a bad man!' the wife said. 'Now he has gone to hell.'

With a wave, they rode out as fast as they could.

'Now let's get fresh horses, too,' Hank said. 'We'll set all of the others free, which will deprive our pursuers of fresh mounts and will buy us more time.'

The horses were snorting with fear after the explosion and it took all of Hank's skills as a horseman to calm two down and transfer their saddles and bridles to them.

'One thing is sure,' Helen said as she mounted and held the reins of Hank's horse while he drove all of the others away. 'They will know where we are.'

'Exactly! And they will know where we are headed. We're going to lead them to the real law.'

13

With fresh horses they put several miles between them and the burning trading post before they finally stopped for breakfast and a very welcome mug of coffee each.

'I can still hardly believe that Macgregor was one of their gang,' Helen said when they were once again on the trail.

'It was only when I was in the jail that I realized it myself,' Hank explained. 'The sheriff was drinking one of his bottles. That probably didn't mean much, but I figured that the only reason that Silver would have known about us was if someone had been following us from the trading post. And then when I saw that he was wearing Dusty, the wrangler's ring I knew that he was one of them. That's why he tried to kill us.'

'So you think they will try to kill us if they catch up?'

'Of course.'

'But why do you think that Sheriff Tyson in Hastings Fork will believe us?'

'He'll certainly believe you. The important thing is to make sure that we get to Hastings Fork before them. If we can persuade him that Silver, Sheriff Slade and the judge are nothing but a bunch of murdering crooks who were working hand in hand with Macgregor at his trading post, then he will contact the US marshal and bring them to justice.'

'But what if you can't persuade him?'

'Then he'll believe them that I am an escaped criminal due to be hanged. In that case — '

'Don't, Hank!' Helen said sharply, concern in her eyes. 'Don't say any more. I won't allow that to happen.'

Hank smiled at her and they rode on in silence. He wondered if she was starting to have some sort of feelings for him.

He already knew that he had fallen in love with her.

$$\star \quad \star \quad \star$$

It took the better part of a whole day to reach Hastings Fork. They camped at night and allowed themselves an hour of sleep in turn, before starting again.

Sheriff Tyson was not in his office when they finally rode in, so they stabled their horses with Henry Masterson, the bow-legged livery owner, then went to Annabelle's, Hastings Fork's best eatery, for a proper meal. They were just finishing their second cup of coffee when Sheriff Tyson found them.

'I heard from Henry Masterson that you were back safely,' he said, sitting down and calling to Annabelle, the homely proprietor for a fresh pot of coffee. 'Did you have any luck?'

Together they told him of all the events that had occurred. Through it all the sheriff sat listening with an expression of mounting incredulity.

Finally, he picked up his coffee cup, which he had allowed to grow cold, and took a gulp. He shook his head, then: 'So old Macgregor is dead and he was one of them!'

'He definitely was,' said Hank. 'He was wearing Dusty's ring. Here it is. Maybe one of his family will recognize it if you manage to contact them.'

Sheriff Tyson frowned. 'You should have told me that the man we thought was the Preacher Eli Tabner was really this Dusty.'

'I am sorry about that, sheriff, but I knew that I had to get on their trail as soon as I could. But if you examine Dusty's body I guess you'll find a white mark where he wore that ring.'

The lawman shook his head. 'We buried him yesterday. I guess old Ebenezer Hood the undertaker would just as soon have us change the name on his grave, but I guess we'll have to do things properly and just have to dig him up and check that hand of his.'

He slapped the table then stood up.

'Right now my first task is to telegraph the US marshal and get him to investigate what was happening over at Hope. And I'd better get ready in case these guys show up.'

Hank wiped his mouth with his napkin. 'As for me, I need to see Hiram Charlesworth as soon as I can.'

Helen yawned. 'Well right now, I think I need to sleep for a week.'

The sheriff nodded. 'After what you have been through, that sounds like a sensible idea.' Then, turning to Hank he added, 'Hiram Charlesworth is staying at the King of Diamonds saloon. He's rented a suite of rooms on the ground floor.'

After he had taken his leave and Hank had paid their bill from the wad of bills he kept in his boot, he opened the door for Helen.

'I think I'll go along to the King of Diamonds and attend to my business with Hiram Charlesworth, Helen. Why don't you go to Doctor Johnson's house and get some rest, like you said.'

She held his gaze for a few moments, seemingly on the brink of saying something, but then she thought otherwise. With a wave she crossed the street for Doctor Johnson's house.

Hank made his way up the street to the King of Diamonds saloon. There, the bartender showed him through a back door and pointed along a corridor.

'Mr Charlesworth rented the best suite we have,' he explained. 'He's able to do his business in there.'

Hank knocked on the door and entered upon hearing Hiram Charlesworth's familiar voice calling him to come in.

The Rio Pintos Stagecoach Company boss was sitting on a chaise longue beside the beautiful Laura Darton, the Hastings Fork banker's widow.

'Hank!' he exclaimed, jumping to his feet and crossing the room to shake his hand. 'Boy, am I glad to see you back alive. And Miss Curtis — how is she?'

'She's just fine, Mr Charlesworth — no thanks to you!'

The stagecoach owner's eyes narrowed. 'I don't follow you. What do you mean?'

'You know exactly what I mean,' Hank retorted. 'So you can drop all the pretence. You sent me and Helen off, sure in the ability of Silver, Wilson and the judge to dispose of us.'

Hiram Charlesworth darted a glance at Laura Darton. 'Mrs Darton, I don't know what he's talking about. This is so embarrassing. I think the poor fellow has taken leave of his senses.'

'Don't give me that,' said Hank, stiffly. 'You, Macgregor and those crooks have been in on all this together. I reckon you have been sabotaging the other stage companies and all of you have grown rich.'

He looked distastefully at the banker's widow. 'And judging by what I see now, I reckon that the latest dry gulching at Devil's Knee was planned to both steal the bank's money and give you an excuse to murder Lester Darton. Then you passed it all off as a heart attack that he conveniently had in your presence. Then you and her could be free to do whatever you plan to do.'

'This is nonsense,' Hiram said, raising his hands plaintively.

'It isn't. Your man Sheriff Slade, or Wilson as I first knew him — who is in hell as we speak, by the way — he told me himself. He knew that I had been a lawman. The only person who could have told him that was you!'

There was the sound of a slow handclap and then through a side door walked Silver. He had a gun pointed straight at Hank. Behind him came the source of the handclap. It was Judge Stanley. He was wearing a Stetson instead of his usual top hat, but under his arm he still had his silver-topped cane.

'Bravo, Hank! Bravo! You seem to have worked it all out,' the judge said. 'Only now we are going to take you back to Hope — draped over a horse.'

Silver laughed. 'Yes, you were shot trying to escape — again.'

'Sheriff Tyson knows all about you,' Hank said. 'He's a proper sheriff, by the way. He is telegraphing for a US marshal at this moment.'

The judge smiled. 'You are a murderer, Hank, and we are respectable citizens of Hope. I am the town mayor and a judge and Silver here is a well-known and liked gambler. Since you murdered our town sheriff, I have appointed him as Hope's new sheriff. Imagine our horror when we found that you had also murdered Finlay Macgregor.'

He shook his head. 'No, I don't think we'll have any trouble in persuading the local sheriff and a US marshal that you are a convicted murderer.'

Hiram Charlsworth spoke up. 'Take him someplace else and kill him, boys. We don't want any of this to be associated with Laura and myself. That fool of a sheriff, Cole Tyson, seems a tad too suspicious about our relationship as it is.'

There was the unmistakeable ratcheting on gun hammers from behind the judge, then a voice called out, 'Drop that weapon, mister. That old fool of a sheriff is right here behind you — and he has heard everything!'

He came into the room, his twin Navy Colts levelled in front of him in unwavering hands.

Judge Stanley turned to him, his cane held halfway along its length.

'Ah, you must be Sheriff Tyson. I am Judge Carlton Stanley. From Hope.'

'And if this jasper in front of you doesn't drop that weapon he'll be beyond hope. He'll soon be riding straight to hell!'

'Sheriff, I can assure you — ' the judge began.

And with a rapid flick of his wrist he darted his cane out and the heavy silver top struck the sheriff between his eyes. It caused him to stagger for a moment, which was enough time for the judge to follow through with two rapid blows with the cane to each of the sheriff's wrists. Both guns fell to the floor. A third blow found the back of Tyson's head and he went down like a poleaxed steer.

'Kill them!' screamed Laura Darton.

Silver had been momentarily distracted and had half-turned, but before he could train his gun again, Hank had drawn and fired.

Silver's body was hurled backwards with a bullet through his black heart.

'Oh my God! Hank!' called Helen, as she rushed into the room. She had been a pace or two behind the sheriff. 'I knew that you were up to something when you said you had to come and find Hiram Charlesworth. I told the sheriff and we came in the back way.'

'Don't worry, Helen, I have them all covered now,' Hank said. 'You just see to the sheriff.'

But with the speed of a rattlesnake Judge Stanley had swung his cane round Helen's throat and he yanked her upright.

'Now you drop that gun or I'll break her neck!' he growled.

Hiram Charlesworth sneered. 'I'd do

it straight away, Hank. The judge here knows how to snap a neck as fast as you can blink an eyelid.'

Hank let his gun drop from his fingers.

'Well what are you waiting for,' Laura Darton screamed. 'Kill them both — now! Before anyone comes.'

But instead, the judge released his grip and pushed Helen roughly aside, so she fell to the floor.

'What are you doing?' snapped Hiram Charlesworth. 'Do as you are told, man!'

But the judge just smiled. He drew his own gun and shot the stagecoach owner in the chest.

'Our arrangement is terminated,' he said, as Charlesworth's body slumped to the floor. 'I have decided, I no longer need any partners.'

He holstered his weapon and then grasped his cane in both hands. He pulled and drew out a silver-topped swordstick. He swished it in the air.

'Well, Hank Hawkins, it is just you

and me now, and two women.'

Laura Darton began to scream.

The judge winced at the noise, drew his gun again and shot her.

'That just makes it you, me and her.' He smiled, totally unconcerned that he had murdered two people in less than ten seconds.

He nodded at Helen where she lay. She was staring up at him with horror.

'So, my friend, my question to you is — do you still think she is worth dying for?'

Hank gave Helen a wan smile, then stood facing the judge who had his sword poised ready to stab him through the chest.

'Yes,' he said. 'Absolutely!' He raised his arms in order to attempt some sort of defence.

'In that case, I think you are about to really find out.' And he drew his sword arm back to thrust for Hank's heart.

There was the explosive noise of a gunshot and the judge was jolted. He looked down, a look of perplexity on his face as he saw a rapidly expanding patch of red on his front. Then he felt forward on his face.

Helen was holding one of Sheriff Tyson's Navy Colts in her hand. The barrel was smoking.

'Helen! You saved me!' Hank gasped. 'And now there . . . there is something I have to tell you.'

She cocked the gun again, this time turning and pointing it directly at his chest. Tears welled up in her eyes.

'I know, Hank. I have known all along. You talked in your sleep when you were delirious for those two days at Doctor Johnson's house. You told me — everything!'

He stared at her in horror. Then he slowly shook his head.

'In that case, Helen, I can't tell you how sorry I am. You have every right to pull that trigger and finish this right here and now.'

He raised his arms from his sides and closed his eyes as he waited for oblivion.

'I . . . I can't, Hank,' she stammered. 'I wanted to once. I had it planned in my mind, but after all that we have been through, I think, I think . . . Perhaps, one day.'

There was a groan and Sheriff Tyson woke and looked round in bewilderment and horror at all of the carnage around them.

Then there was a tentative knocking on the door and concerned and alarmed voices.

'What in the name of tarnation just happened?' the sheriff asked as he retrieved one of his Navy Colts from the floor and accepted the other from Helen.

'To be honest, sheriff, we're not sure,' Hank replied.

'We . . . we think we have found hope,' Helen added as she stood up and reached out for Hank's hand.

We do hope that you have enjoyed reading this large print book.

Did you know that all of our titles are available for purchase?

We publish a wide range of high quality large print books including:
Romances, Mysteries, Classics
General Fiction
Non Fiction and Westerns

Special interest titles available in large print are:
The Little Oxford Dictionary
Music Book, Song Book
Hymn Book, Service Book

Also available from us courtesy of Oxford University Press:
Young Readers' Dictionary
(large print edition)
Young Readers' Thesaurus
(large print edition)

For further information or a free brochure, please contact us at:
Ulverscroft Large Print Books Ltd.,
The Green, Bradgate Road, Anstey,
Leicester, LE7 7FU, England.
Tel: (00 44) **0116 236 4325**
Fax: (00 44) **0116 234 0205**

McANDREW'S STAND

Bill Cartright

Jenny McAndrew and her two sons live in the valley known as McAndrew's Pass. When they hear that the new Rocky Mountains Railroad Company has plans to lay a line through the valley — and their farm — they are devastated at the prospect of their simple lives being destroyed. Clarence Harper, the ruthless boss of the railroad company, is not a man to brook opposition. But in the McAndrews, he finds one family that will not be bullied into submission . . .